WHAT KA

'Let's make tonight one to remember,' said Katy and kissed him.

Dave ran his hands over her breasts and felt the hard nipples through her shirt and the thin cotton bra underneath. He unbuttoned the shirt and tugged it off, then he pushed her bra up over her full breasts and put his mouth to her nipples. They were as hard as cherry pits.

Katy moaned with pleasure. She might be about to dump Dave but not before he gave her what she so badly needed . . .

What Katy Dunn Did

Holly Delatour

HEADLINE DELTA

First published in 1994
by HEADLINE BOOK PUBLISHING

A HEADLINE DELTA paperback

10 9 8 7 6 5 4 3 2 1

ISBN 0 7472 4567 3

Phototypeset by Intype, London

Printed and bound in Great Britain by
Cox & Wyman Ltd, Reading, Berks

HEADLINE BOOK PUBLISHING
A division of Hodder Headline PLC
338 Euston Road,
London NW1 3BH

For Robin

PART ONE

PART ONE

1

The first time that Katy Dunn arrived in London, she was seventeen, a virgin, had come first in her year at secretarial college and was on her way to a job interview with a major oil company located on the south bank of the River Thames.

The job was in the typing pool, and Katy had prepared herself carefully for the interview. Her long, thick, blonde hair was brushed until it gleamed, and her make-up was a dream of understatement; just a touch of mascara outlining the duck-egg blue of her eyes, a thin layer of foundation on the creamy skin of her cheeks and a faint hint of pink lipstick on her full, sensuous mouth that perfectly matched the colour of the nail varnish that tipped the long fingers of her shapely hands. She'd taken equal care with her clothes, and wore sheer black tights over M&S white cotton knickers, a white bra, a white shirt, a charcoal two-piece suit from Next and low-heeled black pumps. She wore low heels because she was a statuesque five foot nine in her stockinged feet and didn't want to tower over everyone at the interview.

Before she left home that morning, and after checking herself in the mirror in her tiny bedroom, she was convinced that she would get the job and would soon shake off the dust of the small town near Bristol where she lived with her mother, father and twin brother, Keith.

Only two things rankled as the fast train from Bristol Temple Meads approached the outskirts of London *en route* to Paddington.

One was that her father had insisted that she be met at the station. The second was her virginal state.

Not that she hadn't been to London before. She had many times. But never alone. Previously she had always been accompanied by family members, or on a school trip, and she'd been looking forward to having a look 'round the capital before the interview, which was due to start at two p.m. That was precisely why she'd caught the fast train that arrived just before eleven, and not one of the slower ones that would have deposited her in town closer to the time of her interview.

'But, Daddy,' she'd protested, 'if I'm to work in London I'm sure to be there on my own eventually.'

'But not on the day of your interview,' he said. 'You never know, you might get lost.' And secretly he hoped that she wouldn't get the position, and would give up the idea of leaving home and settle down to a job in Bristol or Bath.

'Rubbish,' she said, interrupting his thoughts. 'I'm a big girl now. I'll just take a cab.'

But her father put his foot down and contacted cousin Mark. Cousin Mark, or second cousin Mark as he really was, but that was a bit of a mouthful, had lived in London for years. He was almost forty, divorced, had a flat somewhere in south London, worked for an advertising agency in Oxford Street and, as it transpired, was on holiday the week of Katy's interview and was staying in town to do some DIY on his flat. When Katy's father had phoned him he'd agreed, if somewhat reluctantly, to meet Katy outside the Tie Rack shop on the concourse at Paddington at eleven, take her to lunch and deliver her safe and sound in plenty of time for her interview. Then all she had to do was hail a cab back to the station when it was finished and catch a train to Temple Meads, having phoned from Paddington with the time of its arrival, and her father would pick her up in his car.

'Damn cousin Mark,' she said to herself as she stood up to rescue her Burberry raincoat from the luggage rack as the train slowed on its approach to the end of the journey. She hadn't seen him for six or seven years and couldn't remember much about him except that he'd teased her about her height and lack of weight at the time. Things *have* changed she thought as she caught her reflection in the window of the train as it pulled up to the platform. Now her breasts and hips were full, though her waist was still narrow, and the gawky legs that once had driven her crazy were long and shapely with lush thighs that seemed to go on forever. She knew from the glances that she got from the men in the carriage that she was supremely desirable and the knowledge made her sticky between her legs and gave her a warm glow in her tummy.

If only I weren't a virgin, she thought. What a waste of a lovely body.

Not that she hadn't had offers. An abundance in

fact. But she'd just never found anyone who measured up to her idea of the man who would be first to plunder the treasure chest that was hidden by the blonde pelt between her legs. She had often caught her friends' fathers looking at her lustfully, and the husbands where she babysat to earn a little extra pocket money, even the tutors at the college who were charged with taking care of the students they taught. She knew that given half a chance they too would spread her legs and force themselves into the soft, wet paradise that they found there. She knew they all wanted to get into her knickers and pump her pussy full of their seed, but none of them came up to scratch. And besides, she also knew that if she gave in to any of their lustful advances, soon word would get round, and how her reputation would suffer from the gossip.

That was another reason she wanted to move up to London, so that she could have the freedom to meet some real men and find one to whom she could give her greatest gift.

Not that Katy didn't have a boyfriend, she did. Dave was his name. But that was all he was, a mere boy, and although they had petted heavily she would never let him remove her knickers and penetrate her secret place.

And the sad thing, she thought as she disembarked and walked up the platform towards the ticket barrier, is that I love men. I love being with men, much more than with women. And I love their bodies. Looking at them and touching them. And I love cocks, even though the only ones I've ever seen are Dave's and Keith's. Much as she liked Dave, and the feel of his knob in her hand and mouth, she wouldn't let him go all the way. She was determined to save herself for the right man.

And the right man was definitely not Dave. Even though she was fond of him, and surprised him the first night they went out together by giving him a blow job and swallowing his juice. What a shame I won't give in to him and let him fuck me, she thought. It drives him mad that I won't. But it will never happen. Because then he'll want to get married and keep me down in the sticks like a country mouse, when all I want to do is move up to London and see something of life. Not that I will today, lumbered with boring old cousin Mark, and she gave her ticket to the miserable-looking ticket collector and went looking for the Tie Rack.

2

For one brief moment she thought of cutting and running. Getting lost in the metropolis and finding her own way to the interview. But she knew that her father would be furious if she did, and besides she was a good-hearted girl and knew that cousin Mark had given up part of his precious holiday to help her, so she dismissed the thought from her mind.

As she pressed through the barrier she saw the shop she was looking for on her right, and the man standing outside. He was tall, with thick black hair, wearing a dark blue coat open over a grey suit. As she got closer she recognised him as her second cousin, but when she'd last seen him, she'd never noticed how handsome he was.

God, he's gorgeous, she thought as she got closer.

Mark Charles MacDonald to give him his full name hadn't exactly jumped at the chance of meeting Katy. He remembered her as a lanky thing, with long, dishwater-coloured hair pulled back into a ponytail who'd hardly said a word the last time they'd met at some family function or other. And when her father had called out of the blue a few weeks earlier, and explained the problem, in a moment of weakness he'd agreed to get her from Paddington to Waterloo and her interview, and had regretted it ever since. Stupid girl, he thought. Can't she get across London without an escort? Is she simple?

That morning he'd ignored the painting that he should have been doing in his sitting room, shaved, dressed as if for work, and endured the smelly tube train ride across the centre of town.

Where the devil is she? he thought. The damn train should have arrived ten minutes ago.

He watched a blonde dream walking towards him across the concourse, and looked behind her for Katy, when she came right up to him and said, 'Mark?'

He did a classic double take. 'Katy?' he said in disbelief. 'Is that you?'

'The one and only,' she replied.

'It can't be. You've changed . . .'

'Haven't we all?' Katy said.

God, she's beautiful, Mark thought, and instinctively leaned down and kissed her on the cheek.

Katy smiled up at him, he even smells gorgeous she thought. Why didn't anyone tell me?

'Would you like a coffee?' stuttered Mark. 'And then we can choose somewhere for lunch. I honestly didn't recognise you. I thought you were a model going to a shoot.'

'I'd love a coffee,' replied Katy. 'But I don't know about the model bit.'

'Believe me. I work with them all the time.' And he took her arm and led her to the café-bar on the concourse. Even through the material of her raincoat, her jacket and the blouse beneath, his touch thrilled Katy to the core.

9

When they got inside the café, Mark ordered a cappuccino for Katy and a beer for himself, and when they were served they took their drinks to an empty table and sat down.

'Your interview's at two I believe,' said Mark.

'That's right,' agreed Katy.

'At Waterloo.'

She nodded. And mentioned the name of the oil company.

'I know the building,' said Mark. 'I live close by and there's a decent Italian restaurant not far away. Do you like Italian?'

Right then, Katy would have eaten anything to be with Mark, and he would have eaten anything to be with her.

'I love it,' she said.

'Fine. Do you want to take the tube or get a cab?'

'Tube,' said Katy. 'I'd better get used to it if I'm going to move up here.'

'Tube it is then,' said Mark. 'We can be there in less than half an hour.'

They finished their drinks, made their way to the tube station and went to Waterloo. The train was less crowded than when Mark had travelled to Paddington earlier, but it could have been packed to the doors for all he cared, so attracted to Katy was he. And as for her, the novelty of riding on the underground, especially with Mark for company, made the noisy, stuffy trip a pleasure.

They walked from the station to the restaurant, where Mark was obviously well known, and were shown to a secluded table for two in one corner. Their waiter made a special fuss of Katy, drawing back her

10

chair and placing her napkin in her lap with a flourish.

'You must come here a lot,' said Katy. 'Is this where you bring your girlfriends?'

'Sometimes,' replied Mark. 'But I haven't been involved with anyone for a long time.'

Katy was pleased when he said that. More pleased than she should have been, she knew.

'I don't believe it,' she said.

'Why's that?'

'You're a very attractive man. I would have thought you'd have no trouble getting as many girlfriends as you wanted.'

Mark touched her hand, and she felt a thrill again. A thrill that started in her tummy and went down to her cunt in a warm, liquid rush that lubricated her vagina and soaked the gusset of her panties.

'Thank you for the compliment,' he said. 'But sometimes it's a long wait for the right person to come along.'

I'm here, thought Katy. Ready and waiting.

'How about you?' Mark went on. 'I bet there must be queues of young men beating a path to your door.'

'There is someone,' she replied, and Mark felt his heart sink. 'But it's not serious. He's such a stick-in-the-mud. I want to move up to London and he wants to stay at home. If I get this job, I don't think we'll see very much of each other in the future.'

Then I hope you get it, thought Mark. And he was surprised at the strength of his reaction.

'Do you want wine?' he asked, when their waiter came back to take their order.

'Better not,' replied Katy. 'I don't want to go to the interview drunk.'

'Of course not,' said Mark. Katy ordered Perrier and he asked for a beer.

They ate a simple but delicious meal of pasta and salad. Katy drank water throughout, and Mark had another beer. They talked together easily about Katy's interview, her time at college and her hopes for her career; about Mark's job and his flat. As they spoke they both felt their mutual attraction growing.

When the plates were cleared away they ordered coffee, and Mark asked for a brandy. 'Where are you going to live when you come up here?' he asked.

'I haven't got a clue,' said Katy. 'I haven't really thought. There is the small matter of the interview to be considered first.'

'You'll walk it,' said Mark confidently.

'I hope the interview panel is as convinced as you are,' said Katy, 'and I wish I was too.'

'They'd be crazy not to take you on.'

'Thanks,' said Katy. 'If I do get the job I suppose I'll have to come up to London and look around for somewhere.'

'It's not going to be easy,' said Mark. 'How about this?' He paused. 'Have you got any friends in London to stay with while you're looking?'

Katy shook her head.

'Well,' he went on, 'my flat is just 'round the corner. Very central. Why don't you make it your base whilst you're looking for somewhere. Come up and stay for a few days. Longer if you like. I've got a spare room you can have for as long as you need it. Otherwise you'll have to stay in a bed and breakfast or a hotel, which will be expensive. What do you say?'

Katy couldn't believe what she was hearing. 'I think

it's a wonderful idea,' she said. 'I was terribly worried about finding somewhere. Mum and Dad are a bit out of touch in that respect. They'd be bound to think I'd be mugged or something if I came up here on my own. But if I was staying at your place . . .'

'So you will?' asked Mark. The thought of the beautiful girl sitting opposite him spending time under his roof was more intoxicating than the brandy he was drinking.

'Of course,' replied Katy. 'But I know they're going to draw up a short list today. And that means coming back for another interview before I can be sure of getting the job.'

'Come up the night before and stay over. It's much less stressful than a long journey straight before an interview.'

'Are you sure?' said Katy. 'I'm sure you could find a lot of better things to do with your time than looking after me.' She wanted to make sure that he meant what he was saying and was not just making empty promises.

'Believe me, Katy,' he said leaning across the table and looking deeply into her eyes, 'there's nothing more I'd rather do. I'd be flattered to be seen with you anytime. You just say the word and the place is yours for as long as you want to stay there.'

Katy felt a thrill course through her body and she crossed her legs and squeezed her soaking cunt hard. The idea of spending a night at Mark's flat was almost more than she could bear. Please let me get on the short list, she thought.

She looked at her watch. It was already twenty-five to two. Time had flown whilst they were enjoying their first meal together. 'Look at the time,' she wailed. 'I'll be late. And I'll never get the job if I am.'

'Not at all,' said Mark reassuringly. 'I'll get the bill. There's always loads of cabs going past here on the way to the station. You'll be there in five minutes, tops. Don't worry.'

'I'll just go to the ladies to fix my make-up,' said Katy, as she pushed back her chair, and got up from the table.

Mark signalled for the bill and, along with every other man in the restaurant, watched as Katy made her way to the ladies' room, her hips swinging provocatively inside her tight skirt.

3

Mark was as good as his word. He delivered Katy safe and sound at the oil company's headquarters with plenty of time for her to find the room where the interviews were being held, and with five minutes to spare.

As she left the cab he kissed her on the cheek again and his lips seemed to sear the soft down on her skin.

'Do you want me to wait for you?' he asked.

'You're awfully sweet, but don't bother,' replied Katy. 'I don't know how long I'll be.'

'Sure?'

'Yes. I'll get a cab back to Paddington. It looks like there's loads 'round here. I'll be fine.'

'Call me when you get home. You've got the number haven't you?'

She nodded.

'Let me know that you got back safely and how you got on.'

'I will. Thanks for meeting me, and the lunch and everything.'

'It was a pleasure,' said Mark, and they both smiled at each other, and both felt hidden currents in the smiles.

Katy gracefully exited the cab, and Mark gave the driver his home address and as the taxi pulled away, he watched Katy's figure as she walked up to the front of the building. What a body, he thought. And what a lovely personality. I hope she gets on the short list and comes to stay.

And although he didn't know it, Katy was thinking exactly the same thing as she turned up the steps to the door and waved at the back window of the retreating cab.

The interview went well. Katy faced a panel of four people. Two male, two female. By the time she left it was after three and she thought that she had acquitted herself to the best of her ability. Her marks at college had gone down well, and she was almost sure she would get another interview. As she left, the forewoman of the panel told her that she would hear from the company one way or the other within a week.

After the interview Katy grabbed a cab back across London, phoned her mother from Paddington, filled her in briefly about her day, just leaving out one or two details, and told her the time that the train would reach Bristol.

Later that evening, as promised, she rang Mark. At the sound of his voice she felt her eyes fill with stars and for a moment she could hardly speak. She told him what had happened, and promised to call when she heard from the company. When the call was over cousin Mark found himself holding the receiver tightly and hoping that the call would come soon.

Over dinner her mother, father and Keith quizzed her further about her day, and how she had got on with Mark. She made herself reply in an offhanded manner as if he had made little impression. When she told them of his suggestion that she stay at his place overnight before the second interview if it happened and, later, to stop for a few days if she got the job whilst she was looking for digs, they welcomed the news with relief.

After the meal she phoned Dave to tell him her news. She could tell that he wasn't overjoyed that the interview had gone as well as it had. He asked to see her, and when she agreed he drove over in his old Ford Capri. They went for a drink and afterwards parked in a deserted spot they considered their own. Katy wore a short skirt with just brief, transparent panties underneath, a sweat shirt and no bra. After meeting cousin Mark she was as horny as hell and needed some relief. When the car was parked and the radio was playing something soft, Dave reached over and kissed her. She responded eagerly, closing her eyes and pretending that it was Mark that was holding her and touching her tongue with his. Her body softened and she felt her cunt grow damp as her juices lubricated the soft insides of her crack. Her breasts seemed to swell and grow almost painfully heavy, and her nipples stood up, hard and erect and rubbed equally painfully against the fleecy lining of her sweat shirt.

She'd never felt like this with Dave before. And it occurred to her that if it weren't for the fact that she was fantasising about another man, tonight would have been the night she surrendered her most precious gift to him. But it was that knowledge that stopped her. Mark was the man to deflower her if he wanted to. And she had the feeling that he did. Not that he

17

knew that she was a virgin. That was something she would tell him when it happened. And she knew that it would thrill him as much to be told as it would thrill her to tell him. She couldn't wait. Please God, let me get another interview she thought.

No. Dave was just a tool to scratch the itch she felt between her legs. For a moment she felt bad about using him that way. But the itch was so strong that she put the thought to the back of her mind and concentrated on what his hand was doing as it started to roam under her loose top and weigh the heft of her right breast in his palm. She moaned as he squeezed it. It felt as huge as a melon and more sensitive than she had ever thought possible. As Dave squeezed her nipple between his thumb and forefinger, bolts of pleasure as pure as electric shocks tingled through her chest, and she kissed him brutally and bit at his lips until she was afraid she might draw blood.

Dave responded in kind. He had never known Katy to be so passionate and he loved it. He too thought that this was the night that he'd get into her knickers for the first time. But he was wrong. He ran his hand over her belly, then withdrew it from under her sweat shirt and placed it on her thigh. He pushed his fingers up, under her skirt, towards her soaking pussy which was covered with just the merest wisp of fine lingerie.

She placed her hand against his groin and felt the hardness of his prick, and the heat of the blood that engorged it through the material of his jeans. She stroked the length of his tool, and his hands found the elastic at the legs of her panties, his fingers wormed under them and into her pubic hair. His forefinger discovered her slit and it opened welcomingly to the probing digit. Dave pushed his finger in as far as he could, and Katy felt her cunt muscles grip it tight as if they would never let it go.

'I want to fuck you,' he whispered throatily.

'I know,' she said. 'But we have to wait.'

'No,' he said.

'Yes. I'll suck you off, but make me come first. You know how.'

Oh Jesus he thought. But he withdrew his finger with the sucking sound that Katy adored, and found her clitoris and began to rub 'round its tenderness and tweak at it until she thought she might faint from pleasure.

He rubbed at the hard lump of gristle with the ball of his thumb and Katy lay back on the seat of the car and opened her legs wide. He rubbed harder, and she gripped his arm as she felt herself ready to come. He cruelly pinched her clit and she felt as if the car was going at a hundred miles an hour even though it was parked with the engine switched off. She grabbed at his hand through her clothes, forced it down and cried out as she felt the earth move beneath her. She closed her legs tightly on his hand and hoped that the feeling she was experiencing would never end.

When her long orgasm had passed, Katy let her head loll back against the rest behind her and she smiled at Dave in the dim light from the dashboard. Not bad, she thought. But nothing on what Mark could give me.

'Was that OK?' asked Dave.

She hated it when he asked questions like that. Couldn't he tell? She bet that Mark would know.

'Great,' she said. 'Your turn now.'

'Can't we . . .'

'No. But don't worry, we will soon.' She knew she was lying, but she didn't care. She had a feeling that Dave was soon going to be history. But then nothing lasted forever, and she was going to make him happy within the next few minutes. And he'd get over it. Find a nice girl who wanted to stay in the sticks and Katy would just be a memory. A pleasant memory she hoped, but a memory nevertheless. You're growing girl, she thought. And for some reason the thought made her sad.

She reached down for the zip of his jeans and eased it over the swell of his organ, releasing his hard prick from the confines of his clothes.

She leaned down and took the knob of his cock into her mouth and sucked at the hot hardness of it which smelt of soap and sweat and sex.

She tried to swallow it whole, letting her tongue run up and down the shaft. Dave tensed and put one hand into the thickness of her hair at the back of her neck to make sure she didn't stop doing what she was doing. She didn't mind. She loved to suck cock. And she was dying to get Mark's prick into her mouth. Just the thought of his shaft between her teeth almost made her bite into the soft hardness of Dave's weapon.

She sucked and sucked and stroked his balls until she felt his scrotum almost bursting with unreleased come. Then she put the tip of her tongue in his hole, and gently wanked the fat sausage of flesh between his legs.

I wonder what Mark's cock looks like? she thought,

as Dave's whole body jerked and he released a jet of hot, salty jism into her mouth.

4

Katy got the letter summoning her for the second interview two days later. She was asked to attend at the oil company's offices the following Monday at four p.m. She was overjoyed and read her family the letter over the breakfast table. She knew that her father wasn't too pleased at the thought of losing his daughter to the big city, but he put the best face possible on it, and her mother and Keith seemed as happy at the news as Katy was herself.

'I'll phone Mark later and accept his offer to stay,' she said, and felt her insides turn to water at the thought.

'Yes, dear,' said her mother. 'You do that.'

Katy called the personnel office of the oil company at ten and confirmed her appointment, then tapped out Mark's number with trembling fingers.

He answered on the third ring.

'Mark, it's Katy,' she said.

'You've got the interview,' he said, and the sound of his voice made her go weak at the knees.

'Yes.'

'Well done. I told you didn't I?'

'I haven't got the job yet.'

22

'A mere formality.'

'Thank you,' said Katy.

'How have you been?'

'Fine. You?'

'All the better for hearing your voice. When's the interview?'

'Four o'clock on Monday afternoon.'

'Come up on Sunday. I'll cook dinner. I'm a fair cook if I say so myself. I'm back at work on Monday, but you can have the run of the place when I've gone. I've got a spare front door key. Trouble is I won't be able to see you ... Why not stay Monday night too? We can go out and paint the town red to celebrate. If you'd like that of course.'

'I'd love it. But there may be nothing to celebrate.'

'Of course there will. So will you stay?'

'Yes. I've got nothing to do here since I've left college. I'm just kicking my heels really.'

'Terrific. Now you've got my address, haven't you?'

Katy agreed that she had. In fact she had it off by heart.

'What time train will you get on Sunday?'

'There's a 125 at noon. I'll be with you around two. Is that alright?'

'Wonderful. I can't wait.'

'Nor me,' she said and blushed.

'Do you want me to meet you at Paddington?'

'No. I'll be fine. I may take a cab, or risk the tube. I've got an *A-Z*. I bought one at the station on the way home the other day.'

'You knew you'd get another interview.'

'I was pretty sure. But I didn't want to put a jinx on it.'

'Impossible. So I'll see you when you get here. Take care, and give my love to everyone down there.'

'I'll do that. Goodbye, Mark.'

'Goodbye, Katy. I'll see you on Sunday.' And with that they finished the call.

Katy almost danced into the kitchen where her mother was putting away the clean breakfast dishes.

'I'm going to stay up in London on Sunday and Monday night,' said Katy. 'I'll be able to do some shopping on Tuesday and be back here in the afternoon.'

'Lovely, dear,' said her mother.

'So that's alright?' said Katy. 'The extra day, I mean. It'll give me a chance to have a good look 'round.'

'Of course.'

'Thanks, mum,' said Katy, and kissed her on the cheek and went upstairs to her room. Three days until I see him, she thought as she sat in front of her dressing table mirror and brushed her hair. I can't wait.

5

Sunday dawned bright and warm, and Katy was up early getting ready for her extended trip to London. She packed her interview suit, white blouse, underwear and tights, plus another set of very sexy lingerie and two pairs of seamed nylons. Then for Tuesday, she chose a simple, flower-patterned, button-fronted dress, and finally on top of the rest of her clothes she carefully folded a short, black, see-through lace nightgown, and a white cotton robe. For the journey she dressed in blue jeans, a checked shirt and a leather jacket, and carried her Burberry over her arm. She didn't want to subject Mark to overkill by turning up on a Sunday lunchtime looking like a vamp out of a nineteen-thirties Hollywood movie. But she still paid especial attention to her make-up in her dressing table mirror before she left the house.

· Her father dropped her off at the station in plenty of time, and armed with three or four Sunday papers she found a corner seat in the middle of the train and settled down to wait for the off.

For once, there were no track repairs on the line or other delays, and Katy's train slid into Paddington station dead on time. She stuffed the papers into her bag and went through the ticket gate and out into the sunshine. She debated whether to go back and get the tube, or look for a cab, and finally decided to travel to south London by bus. She bought a travel card at a newsagents and jumped on the first bus that came along going in what she thought was the right direction, and went upstairs to enjoy the view. She only had a hazy idea where she was going, but with the assistance of the conductor, who gave her directions, she changed buses a couple of times, and got to Waterloo by two-fifteen. She walked the last quarter mile or so and, with the help of her *A-Z*, found Mark's street just after two-thirty.

She rang the bell marked 'MacDonald' at his house, and within thirty seconds the door was opened by Mark, who was wearing a pale blue chambray shirt, black jeans and tan boots. Katy thought he looked gorgeous.

'Katy,' he said. 'I was just beginning to worry about you.'

She smiled her thanks. 'No need,' she said. 'I decided to come from Paddington by bus, it's such a lovely day and I didn't think it would take so long.'

'Sunday is not a good day. But you're here now. Come on in. Let me take your bag.'

Mark allowed Katy to enter and followed her upstairs. As they went he couldn't help noticing the way her buttocks moved beautifully in her skin-tight jeans.

He showed her into his flat, which smelt deliciously of cooking food, along the hall and into the living room. It was large and light, decorated in pale cream with a dark brown carpet, a brown three-piece suite, and a four-place dining table laid for two, with a crisp white tablecloth and gleaming cutlery and glasses.

God, thought Katy, who was used to eating off the kitchen table, or her lap in front of the TV at home. This is posh.

One wall of the living room was covered in shelves full of books, vying for room with a TV, video and stereo system, and what looked like a complete collection of Sunday papers was scattered everywhere. Mark rounded them up and piled them on a low coffee table in front of the settee. 'Sorry about that,' he said. 'Business you know. Got to keep up with the competition.'

'Don't worry. It makes the place look comfortable. This is a lovely place,' said Katy, looking 'round in admiration. 'Really nice.'

'I think so,' said Mark. 'I just finished decorating. Now, do you want to see your room or have a drink first?'

'A drink.'

'Tea, coffee, or something stronger? I've just opened a bottle of wine. A Chardonnay. A bit posey I'm afraid, but I like it.'

Katy didn't know what Chardonnay was, but she liked the sound of the name. The only wine she'd ever had was house red or white at a restaurant, or cheap supermarket plonk. 'Wine sounds lovely,' she said.

Cousin Mark dropped her bag on the floor and said, 'The kitchen's out back. Come on through,' and he led her into the hall again, and through another door at the end.

Inside the kitchen the smell of food was even more delicious and made Katy's mouth water. The room was small, and the fittings were all in white wood and white enamel. The window was tiny and gave a good view of the railway sidings at the back of Waterloo Station.

'It can be a bit noisy sometimes,' said Mark, noticing Katy looking through the window. 'That's why my room's at the front. I'm afraid yours isn't. I hope they don't keep you awake.'

'I'm sure they won't,' said Katy. 'I'll probably be too excited to sleep anyway.'

Mark smiled. 'Unless my cooking gives you indigestion.'

'It smells too delicious for that,' said Katy. 'What are we having?'

'It's just a chicken casserole,' said Mark, 'with some new potatoes. I hope you're not a vegetarian.'

Katy shook her head. 'No,' she said.

'Good. Then there's an apricot and peach pie to follow. Sarah Lee, I'm afraid. Fresh out of the freezer.'

'Sounds smashing,' said Katy.

'That's alright then,' he said, and opened the fridge door and took out a bottle of wine.

'It does smell wonderful,' said Katy, as Mark took a clean glass from a cupboard, putting it on one of the work surfaces next to a partially filled one that he'd obviously been using. He popped the cork out of the bottle and filled both glasses to the brim, and handed her one. 'I'm not a very good cook, I'm afraid,' she said.

'If you live on your own long enough, you have to be. Or survive on takeaways or eat out a lot. You'll learn when you come up to London to live.'

'Or get a charge card at Marks and Sparks,' said

Katy. 'Which sounds more likely.'

Mark smiled again. 'You're like a breath of fresh air in this bachelor flat of mine. Here's to a successful interview tomorrow,' and he touched the rim of his glass to hers.

'Thank you,' replied Katy. 'And thank you again for letting me stay.'

'We'll have a great time,' said Mark. 'Don't you worry.'

I do hope so, thought Katy as she took a sip from her glass. The wine tasted lovely and she said so.

'Good,' he said, refilling her glass. 'I've got another three bottles in the fridge. So when do you want to eat?'

'As soon as you like,' replied Katy.

'Let me show you your room, and while you're unpacking I'll get everything ready. How does that sound?'

'That's fine,' said Katy.

And it was. Mark fetched her bag from the living room and took her around the corner of the hall to a small room that also overlooked the railway sidings. On the way he showed Katy the bathroom and toilet. Her room was pin neat, with a single bed, a chest of drawers and a small wardrobe. 'It's a bit spartan,' he said. 'But I don't have many guests these days.'

'It'll do fine,' said Katy.

'I'll leave you to it then. Lunch will be in about fifteen minutes. OK?'

'Wonderful. I'm starving,' she said.

'That's good. I'll take your glass into the living room. Come in as soon as you're unpacked.'

And he left her alone, closing the door gently

behind him. Katy sat on the bed and thought how perfectly wonderful Mark was. Sexy, and a good cook, she thought. And as he went back to the kitchen he could smell her perfume all through the flat and felt his cock harden slightly as he sipped a drop of wine from the glass that she had used, and tasted her lipstick in his mouth.

She unpacked, and put her underwear into the drawers of the chest, hung her suit, blouse and dress neatly in the wardrobe, and put her nightdress under the pillow, enjoying the sensuous feel of the lace on her skin, then went back to join Mark in the living room.

The meal they ate together was delicious, and before they'd finished the apricot and peach pie, they'd got through two more bottles of wine. Although it must be said that Mark had drunk more than his fair share.

After he had stacked the crockery in the dishwasher and made coffee, Mark sat in the living room with Katy, she on the sofa, he on one of the armchairs opposite. Katy wished that he'd sit next to her, and unbeknown to her he wished that he was sitting next to her too.

The rest of the afternoon and the evening flew by as they chatted together comfortably, and before they knew it, it was after ten.

'I think I'm going to turn in,' said Mark finally, yawning and stretching. 'Work tomorrow.'

'You're right,' said Katy. 'And it's my big day.'

'I shouldn't worry,' said Mark. 'You'll have no problems dazzling the interviewers.'

Mark suggested that Katy use the bathroom first,

and she went in, had a pee and cleaned her teeth, then went to her room, took off her jeans, shirt and underwear, and put on the nightie she had bought to sleep in. She admired the way that it barely covered her naked image in the mirror of the wardrobe, and twirled so that her pubic bush and bare arse winked at her from under the hem of the garment, giggled, and got into bed. She heard Mark moving around the flat and then he knocked on her door. Her heart jumped at the sound and she called 'Come in.' Was he going to try and make love to her? she wondered. She lay back on the pillows and pulled the sheet up so that it covered her nipples, which were clearly visible through the lace of her bodice, and he entered. He was wearing a dressing gown and his feet and legs were bare. Katy felt herself juicing up as he came over to the bedside.

'I thought I'd give you the spare keys now in case I miss you in the morning. I know your interview's not until late afternoon, so I won't give you a shout. Just sleep in if you want. The Chubb's for the outside door, the Yale's for the flat door,' and he put two keys on a ring on top of the chest of drawers.

'That's very thoughtful of you,' said Katy. 'But I expect I'll be up early. I'll be too excited to sleep in.'

'Just in case then,' said Mark. 'But if I don't see you, good luck.'

'Thank you,' said Katy.

'Good night,' said Mark. 'Sleep well and have sweet dreams,' and he leaned over the bed and kissed her gently on the cheek. Katy wanted to drag him down next to her and tear off his dressing gown, but she didn't dare.

'Until tomorrow, then,' said cousin Mark, and left the room, closing the door softly behind him.

Damn, thought Katy. Why doesn't he do something?

Her naked cunt was hot and sticky beneath the bedclothes, and her breasts were swollen, the nipples as hard as stones. She put her right hand up to her right breast and squeezed it gently through the lace of her nightdress. She moaned softly to herself as she massaged the warm flesh and opened her legs wide and put the fingers of her left hand down into her pubic hair, finding her wet crack and the swollen clitoris that peeked out from its hood of skin. She ran her middle finger around the tiny erection and moaned again with pleasure. Mark, she thought. I wish it was your fingers that were touching my cunt, and your hand on my tit, and she squeezed the globe of flesh harder through the lace, then freed it from the restraint of her nightie and tweaked her nipple hard. Her fingers moved faster on her clitoris and she slid two of them up the length of her aching tunnel and found the delicate G-spot and massaged it until she was writhing all over the bed, frightened that Mark would hear and come and investigate, although that was really what she wanted most of all. For him to come in and find her masturbating and finish the job with his prick.

Finally, she could stand it no more and allowed an orgasm to wrack her body, pushing her face into the pillow to disguise her moans of delight.

Meanwhile, Mark had gone to his room and taken off his dressing gown. Underneath he was naked. He had seen Katy's discarded white knickers in her bedroom, and the sight had sent the blood rushing to his penis again. Why didn't I just kiss her properly? he thought as he slid beneath the covers of his bed. The feel of the smooth sheets on his prick hardened it still further and he felt his balls swell as they filled with hot spunk. He put his hand down and felt the hairs on his scrotum rise as he stroked them gently and took the shaft of his cock in his right hand. His prick was fully erect by now and felt huge in his palm, and he rubbed the length of it and thought of Katy's body, luscious in the lace of her nightie, and he bit his lip as he started to wank himself off. He tightened his grip on the length of his weapon, and moved it up and down as he dreamed of opening Katy's legs and plunging himself into the luxury of her pussy. He imagined the hot wetness of her insides grasping him, and he too writhed about the bed, little knowing that just a few yards away she was doing exactly the same.

'Katy,' he whispered to himself, as the strokes of his wank got shorter and faster. 'Katy, my love,' and as he felt his sperm ready to shoot, he reached for a handful of tissues from the box that he kept by his bed, and he turned, arching his body as he did so, and shot his load into them, then fell back, fully spent but unsatisfied, onto the softness of his mattress.

6

Katy was surprised to find that when she opened her eyes the next morning it was already past nine o'clock. She got out of bed, slid her robe on over her nightie and left her room. The flat was silent and empty. She went to the bathroom, relieved herself and cleaned her teeth, then into the kitchen where she switched on the still warm kettle to boil. On one of the work surfaces was a note. It read:

Dear Katy,
It's now eight forty-five and I'm leaving for work. There's milk in the fridge, coffee and tea in the cupboard. The bread in the bin is Saturday's I'm afraid, but there's a bakery on the corner if you want fresh. Turn right outside the front door. Help yourself to anything else you fancy to eat.

Good luck with the interview this afternoon. Why don't you call me at my office and let me know how you get on? Number on card attached. Treat the place as your own today, and I'll see you later.

Love, Mark

There was one of Mark's business cards pinned to the note. Katy smiled at his thoughtfulness, and when the kettle clicked off she made herself a cup of tea, found the remains of the loaf in the bread bin and put two slices in the toaster. She took butter from the fridge and a pot of marmalade from the cupboard, and when her breakfast was ready, she sat and read some more of yesterday's papers at the kitchen table as she ate.

She spent the rest of the morning pottering around the flat, singing along to the radio, and after she warmed up a tin of soup which she drank with more toast for her lunch, had a long soak in the bath, got herself ready for the interview and presented herself at the oil company's HQ at four o'clock precisely. The original candidates seemed to have been cut down to a short list of half a dozen or so from what Katy could gather, and she only had a brief wait before she was seen by the same panel as at her previous interview. She felt that it went very well and this time, when the interview was over, she was asked to wait in a small ante-room.

After ten minutes or so, one of the two women interviewers popped her head round the door and invited Katy to go to her office where she informed her that the company was very pleased to offer her a position as a junior secretary beginning the very next Monday morning at nine-thirty a.m.

Delighted, Katy accepted the offer and after a brief conversation she left the offices with full details of where and to whom she should report on her first morning at work.

It was a beautiful afternoon, made even more so by

Katy's good news, and she almost danced along the street outside as she searched for a phone box to call Mark at his office.

'I told you, didn't I?' he said, when she got through and told him the news.

'Yes you did.'

'I'm so pleased for you Katy,' he said. 'Let's go out tonight and celebrate. I'll buy you dinner. Would you like that?'

'Nothing I'd like more,' said Katy. 'That's very kind of you.'

'Not at all. It's a pleasure. I'll see you back at the flat in a little while. I'm not sure what time. Things are a bit hectic here, but I'll be as quick as I can. What are you going to do about accommodation by the way?'

'I don't know,' said Katy, who hadn't really considered the matter in her excitement at getting the job. 'I thought I'd have more time to look round.'

'Well, we can't have you sleeping in a cardboard box, can we? Why don't you stay at my place next week. At least then you'll have the evenings to do some flat-hunting.'

'Thank you,' said Katy. 'You've saved my life.'

'No problem,' said Mark. 'I'll see you later, OK?'

'OK,' said Katy. 'Bye,' and put down the phone.

She caught a cab back to the flat and immediately went into the living room, dumped her handbag on the sofa and phoned home where she spoke to her mother who was also delighted at her news. She told her mother that Mark was taking her out for dinner, and what he had said on the phone about her staying at his flat, and Katy could tell that she was happy that her daughter had somewhere to live whilst she looked for her own place.

'I'll tell your father the minute he gets in from work,' her mother said.

'I hope he'll be happy for me,' said Katy wistfully, already becoming homesick although she hadn't left home yet. Even though it had been her main ambition for months.

'Of course he will, pet,' said her mother, sensing Katy's mood. 'And don't you worry. You're only a couple of hours away, and we'll come and visit you often.'

'Will you, Mum?' said Katy, already cheering up. 'That'll be great. I'd better ring off now. I don't want cousin Mark moaning about the phone bills before I've even moved in.'

'Alright, love,' said her mother. 'Have a good evening and we'll see you tomorrow.' And they made their farewells and rang off.

Although Katy had already taken one bath that afternoon, she wasn't used to the gritty London air and felt grubby again, so decided on a quick shower before getting dressed for dinner. She went to her bedroom, stripped off her interview clothes and went into the bathroom. She didn't bother with her robe as she knew she'd only be a moment. She stood under first the hot spray, then the cold, and in less than two minutes she walked out of the bathroom with the towel wrapped around her nakedness and into the sitting room to get her bag. She found Mark taking off his jacket.

'Hello,' he said. 'Enjoy your shower?'

Katy clasped the towel close to her bosom, aware

of the fact that it was hardly long enough to cover her blonde pussy and reddened. 'I'm sorry,' she said. 'I didn't realise you were in. I just came to get my make-up out of my bag.'

'I arrived a minute ago and heard you splashing around. I was so excited at your news that I just left everything and got a cab back. I didn't want to give you a start. Now I have. I'm sorry.'

'Don't apologise,' said Katy. 'I just wasn't thinking.'

'May I ask you a question?' said Mark.

'Of course. What?'

'Now that you're moving in for a while, are you going to make a habit of walking around like that in front of me?' As he spoke, his eyes roved up and down her body until she thought that she would faint with the pressure of them on her. Her nipples hardened and her cunt lubricated instinctively at being caught so scantily covered by the man she desired most in the world.

'I'm sorry,' said Katy again. 'Not if you don't want me to. It was an accident. I didn't mean you to see me like this.'

'Don't worry. Feel free to do what you want.' said Mark reassuringly. 'I think it's charming.'

'Do you?' asked Katy. 'Why?'

'Why do you think?' asked Mark. 'Any man would welcome the sight of a nubile female teenager running around his house half naked.'

Katy felt herself blush again, her nipples hardened even more and the delicious warmth between her legs seemed to fill her whole body. 'I'll do it for you as often as you like,' she said boldly. 'I like being admired by handsome men.' And as she blurted out the words, her blush deepened even further until she thought that her skin would burst into flames so hot was it.

'Katy, you're adorable,' said Mark.

'Thank you,' said Katy prettily and bent her knees to pick up her bag so that she wouldn't expose too much of herself to Mark's prying eyes. She wanted him, but she wanted to tease him a little first. She extracted her make-up bag and turned and walked over to the door feeling his gaze on the backs of her bare thighs as she went. 'I'll get dressed,' she said, and turned and gave him her most seductive look. 'I won't be long.'

'Take your time,' said Mark. 'We've got all night.'

If only, wished Katy to herself as she went down the hall.

She entered her room and sat on the bed, took her make-up mirror from out of her bag, propped it on the dresser and began to do her make up. As she carefully painted her face she could hardly control the shaking of her hands from the feelings of desire for her handsome cousin that were racing through her body like rivers of fire. Please come to me Mark, she thought. Oh please come to me and take my maidenhead.

When she was almost finished, and she thought that he hadn't got her message, she heard a tap on the door and with a feeling of triumph and relief called out 'Yes.'

Mark entered the room as Katy made the last fine adjustment to her lipstick and looked up from her reflection.

'Are you decent?' he asked.

'Of course. Come in,' and she stood and faced him,

this time not holding the towel at all. Just allowing the knot she had tied in the corner to hold it in place over her modesty.

'I just wondered where you wanted to go this evening?' He said. 'It's your celebration, so you should choose. Is there any place special you fancy? Anything you particularly want to do?'

She felt like screaming, 'I want to fuck you!' but she didn't dare. Then circumstances took control of the situation. As Katy stood facing Mark, the knot in the towel came undone and it slipped to the floor leaving Katy stark naked before her cousin for the first time. Stark naked before any man, apart from her brother Keith, since she'd reached puberty in fact. Although Dave had seen her breasts and thighs, she'd never actually stripped off completely before him, being afraid of the consequences. Instinctively she covered her bush and breasts and felt herself blush again, this time a deep crimson as the blood rushed to the surface of her skin.

Mark stood before her. 'You're quite beautiful,' he said.

Katy couldn't believe her ears. It was beginning to happen just as she had dreamed. 'Am I?' Was all she could gasp through dry lips that longed to be kissed.

'Yes. Can I see you?'

She blushed an even deeper red and felt quite faint at his words. He did want her. She knew that he did. She nodded, and removed her arms from across her body and allowed his eyes to rove over her figure. She stood proudly, her belly churning, her pussy dripping juices down her thighs and the tips of her breasts, swollen and painful with desire.

'Quite beautiful. I knew you would be,' said Mark.

'Thank you,' she said.

'I want to make love to you,' he said, and his words were like the sweetest music she had ever heard.

'I've wanted to make love to you since we met again after all that time, the other day. I think about you constantly,' Katy breathed.

'I think about you too.'

'Do you?'

'Every minute.'

'I'm glad. There's just one thing you should know.' He looked puzzled. 'What?'

'I-I'm a virgin,' she stuttered.

'A virgin,' he echoed. 'I-I—.' Now it was his turn to stutter.

'What?' asked Katy.

'I never thought . . . I assumed.'

'Does it make a difference?' she asked.

He shook his head. 'No. Of course not. But are you sure you're ready?'

'Yes,' cried Katy. 'I want it to be you that takes my virginity, Mark. Say that you will. I want you to be the first man to make love to me.'

'Of course I will, my darling,' said Mark reassuringly. 'I think it's wonderful that you've saved yourself just for me. And thank you for telling me before and not later. I'll be sure to be gentle.'

Katy felt her knees go weak again, and then weaker still as Mark took off his tie and began to unbutton his shirt. She watched entranced as he pulled the bottom of it out of his trousers and slid it off his shoulders. What a beautiful chest he has, she thought. Firm and muscled with a sheen of dark body hair

41

from nipple to nipple. She ached to touch it, but waited. Mark eased off his shoes and put one foot up after the other to remove his socks. When Katy looked at his groin she could see the material of his trousers tent up as his erection grew.

Mark undid the button on his waistband and slid down the zip, pushed his trousers over his hips, stepped out of them and kicked them away. Then he put his thumbs under the elastic of his patterned boxers. He looked at Katy. 'Are you really sure?' he asked.

'I've never been so sure of anything in my life,' she said calmly, but inside she was screaming: Don't stop! Don't stop! Let me see your penis and find out if it's as beautiful as I've dreamed.

Mark smiled and forced his pants over his hips and the length of his prick.

First of all Katy saw the tangle of dark pubic hair and then his cock popped into view, standing erectly away from the hard sacs of his balls. He dropped the shorts to the floor, and stepped out of them.

Katy looked unashamedly at the beautiful weapon of love that reared up from Mark's groin. It's wonderful, she thought. Just like I'd dreamed it would be. Eight. No, ten inches at least of prime meat that looks like it could be a Greek god's. And all for me.

They stood a yard from each other, naked for the first time. Lovers who had never even kissed properly. Mark moved towards Katy and gathered her up in his arms and kissed her. She felt the hard beauty between his legs poke into her belly then slide up parallel to their bodies, to the bottom of her breasts which were squashed against Mark's manly chest.

The kiss seemed to last for hours, but end in a

second. It was the most wonderful kiss that Katy had ever experienced and she knew that she would remember it forever.

Mark led her slowly over to her bed, pulled back the covers and lowered her gently to the mattress, then lay next to her and kissed her again. Their kisses grew in length and intensity, and Katy felt the need in her womb almost like a pain as her cunt muscles clenched and unclenched with the desire to be filled with his hot, hard meat.

Mark lowered his head to her breasts and took her right teat in his mouth. He ran his tongue around the aureole and felt the tiny lumps and bumps on it, and her nipple grew in his mouth. He sucked at the hard nub of gristle and felt her tense beneath him. He slid her breast out of his mouth and ran his tongue down her belly and into the roughness of her pubic hair, and down further until he tasted her juices and it slid into her cunt smoothly. He licked around the inside of her, and she opened her legs wide to allow his mouth the freedom to rove around her delicious wet box. When he removed his mouth from her cunt and moved up to kiss her mouth again she greedily sucked her own juices off his lips.

'Have you ever kissed a man's cock?' he whispered.

She nodded.

'Whose?'

'My ex-boyfriend's at home.'

'Isn't he your boyfriend any more?'

'No.' Katy knew that that episode was now over forever.

Mark didn't enquire further. 'Did you like it?'

She nodded.

'Did you swallow his come?'

She blushed once more, and nodded again.

'Did you let him touch you between your legs?'

Katy responded with another nod.

'With his mouth?'

'Sometimes,' said Katy.

Mark smiled at the thought. 'Did you like it?'

'Not as much as when you touch me and kiss me there.'

'That's nice. But you wouldn't let him fuck you. Why not?'

'He wasn't the right man to have my virginity.'

'And I am?'

She nodded for a fourth time. 'I knew you were immediately I saw you waiting for me at the station.'

'You're wonderful.'

'Will it hurt?'

'What?'

'When you fuck me.'

'Maybe for a second. But don't worry, I'll be as gentle as I can be.'

'I know you will,' said Katy, and they kissed deeply again.

'Suck *me*,' said Mark.

Katy moved around on the bed and she put her head between Mark's legs. She lifted up the huge root of his sex and closed her gorgeous lips over it. She sucked the great thing down her throat and tongued the top until Mark almost screamed in ecstasy. He lay back against the pillow and enjoyed the sensation of a virgin sucking him off before he deflowered her, and his prick grew even bigger and harder under her ministrations.

44

Finally, he could bear it no more and he pulled her up beside him, rolled her onto her back and mounted her. He felt his helmet rub against the roughness of her pubes and he said, 'Put me inside you.'

Katy reached down and pushed the head of his cock between the lips of her cunt, and he felt the silky smoothness of the inside of her love tunnel. He pushed down, slowly but firmly, and to Katy it felt as if she was being invaded, and she almost pushed him away, before a knife of pain cut like a scythe through her belly and she gasped, before the pain turned to a warmth that seemed to permeate her whole being and the feeling of invasion turned to one of wholeness as Mark became part of her.

She lay with him on top of her, his body supported by his elbows so as not to be too heavy, and he began to move inside her cunt. Every rub of his cock inside her tunnel was like an electric shock in her brain, and she forgot about everything except their sexual love, as she began to move with him in perfect synchronisation with the strokes of his prick.

This is as wonderful as I always dreamed it would be, she thought, as Mark slowly screwed her arse into the mattress. Their mouths were glued together in long sensual kisses as they made love and, suddenly, for the first time, Katy felt an orgasm growing inside her from a real fuck. She pulled Mark down so that the weight of his body was on top of hers, and she hoped that he'd squash her to death. She raked her nails down his spine and his strokes became faster, his balls, heavy with come, banging against the crack between her buttocks. She lifted her legs and locked her ankles together behind his hips and gave herself totally to the sensualism of the act.

'I'm going to come,' he grunted in her ear.

'Yes,' she cried. 'Yes! Yes! Yes!' And as he stiffened, his cock bucked inside her and she felt his hot spunk erupt up into her womb, she allowed the waves of her orgasm to wash over her too.

7

Mark collapsed onto Katy's body and they lay together, sticky with sweat, saliva and the juices of their mutual come. Katy held Mark tightly, not wanting to lose the magnificent feeling of his body on hers. Eventually his cock shrank inside her and he rolled off her supine form and lay gasping for breath on the bed covers next to her. He found her hand with his and squeezed it tightly. 'That was marvellous,' he said.

'Wonderful,' she breathed. 'I love you, Mark.'

'And I love you too, Katy,' he said, and lifted his head and they kissed again.

She put her hand down and touched his cock, which immediately started to grow again under the tips of her fingers. She looked down at it and said in surprise, 'It's all bloody. I haven't hurt you have I?'

Mark sat up and examined himself. 'So it is,' he said. 'Let me look at the sheets.' And he pushed her bottom and she moved aside. She saw Mark smile as he examined the sheet where she'd been lying when they made love. 'A real virgin,' he said. 'Did I hurt *you*?'

'Only for a second at the start.'

'That was your hymen breaking.'

'Really.' Katy looked down and saw that she'd been lying in a pool of mixed blood and jism. 'I told you, didn't I?'

'I'm so proud of you,' said Mark.

'Can we do it again?' asked Katy shyly.

'Again and again. As many times as you want,' said Mark.

'Now.'

'Whenever you want.'

'I want it now,' said Katy. 'I can't wait.'

'Shall we go into my room? The bed's bigger there,' said Mark. 'More room to roll around and stretch out.'

'Can I sleep with you tonight?' asked Katy.

'Of course.'

'That's wonderful. I've never spent the night with a man before.'

'Katy, you're adorable,' said Mark. 'But what about dinner?'

'Can we send out for a pizza?' said Katy naughtily. 'I've got to go home tomorrow and I want to make love to you all night.'

'You'll wear me out,' said Mark. 'I'm not as young as you.'

'I'll make you young,' said Katy. 'Come on. I want to fuck you again.' And she jumped out of bed and ran out of the door towards Mark's room, and he followed her closely behind.

Katy had looked inside Mark's bedroom that morning when she'd been alone in the flat. She couldn't resist the temptation, and he had told her to treat the place as her own in the note he'd left, so she certainly didn't feel bad about looking through his things.

When she'd peeped round the door, she'd been

pleased to see that he had an oversized double bed covered with a duvet in a black cover, black sheets and matching black pillowcases. The bed took up most of the room, leaving just enough space for a small TV set on a table at the foot of the bed, a chest of drawers similar to the one in the room she'd been using and a bedside table that held a lamp, an alarm clock and a telephone.

The far wall consisted of a pair of sliding doors that led to a fitted wardrobe. Katy had pushed the doors open and touched the sleeves of Mark's jackets, then opened the drawers in the chest, and found the neat piles of crisply ironed boxer shorts and T-shirts, and run her fingers across the smooth cotton and silk of the garments and felt her cunt get wet as she thought about them intimately touching his body. She'd lifted the top pair of shorts to her face and sniffed the material that she knew touched his cock and had to wank herself off again, she'd become so horny.

She'd sat on the bed and lay down with her head on the pillow where his head rested at night, and breathed in the faint masculine smell that he'd left on the material of the pillowcase. Her hand had gone between her legs again, and she'd found the tender spot around her clitoris and rubbed at her flesh through the material of her panties. It had only taken a second for her to come, and she lay shaking on Mark's duvet before getting up, straightening the bedclothes and quietly leaving the room.

And now she was there again, and only a moment away from being under the covers of Mark's bed with his cock inside her cunt again.

He burst into the room behind her and shoved her

face down on the bed and dived on top of her body, covering her neck and shoulders with kisses. She squealed in delight and they rolled over together until they were facing each other and their mouths met again and again. For Katy this was true bliss and as they kissed she felt her cunt muscles contract as they longed to grip Mark's prick in their embrace again. He traced the shape of her body with his mouth, kissing every inch of it as he began to get to know its curves intimately. Katy lay beneath his kisses, knowing that her turn to map out his form with her mouth and fingers would come soon. They were alone in the flat with all the time in the world to explore each other, and that thought combined with Mark's touches and kisses opened her pussy wide, and the juices were streaming out of her like a river. She had no idea that her body could produce such lubrication, and for the first time in her life she knew what it felt to be a real woman.

Finally, when she thought that she could bear his kisses and caresses no more without bursting, Mark mounted her again and slid the hard length of his prick into her cunt crack once more. If possible, her second invasion by her cousin's member felt even better than the first. Her love tunnel was wide open and welcoming to his cock, and it felt like hot steel sheathed in velvet as it slid along the length of her. She clasped her lover tightly and their mouths cleaved to each other as they began to move together again.

'Does that feel good?' he asked.

'Wonderful. Better than wonderful. Perfect. I never thought that anything could feel this good.'

'It'll get better I promise,' he said.

50

'Mark, if it gets any better than this I'll die.'

'Don't die too soon. We've got a lot to catch up on. Or at least I have.'

'Take as much time as you like,' she whispered as his strokes became shorter, and he prepared to give her his love juices again.

Katy pushed her hips up against Mark's movements and she could hear the slap, slap, slap of their sweaty bodies as they pushed against each other, and thought that she'd never heard a more beautiful sound in her life. As if by magic she felt the first flowering of an orgasm deep inside her belly where the tip of his penis tickled the entrance to her womb, and she gritted her teeth and moved harder with him. Instinctively he knew what her movements meant and he slammed his cock into her, and she could feel his breath hot and fragrant on her cheek as he bit down on her shoulder, letting loose his eruption of spunk inside her. She allowed herself to come on the length of his knob and sunk her fingernails into his back.

Once again the pair of them lay together, Katy still impaled on Mark's sword, and she gently stroked his spine where she thought she'd probably drawn blood.

'That was heaven,' she said.

'Katy, you're magnificent,' he gasped. 'I'm so glad I've found you.'

They must have lain like that, exhausted from their exertions, for ten minutes or more, as Mark's cock softened inside Katy's cunt until she suddenly felt ravenous and said, 'What about that pizza?'

8

'Fucking sure does make you hungry,' said Mark. Katy loved the way he said 'fucking'. It turned her stomach to mush and made her cunt feel empty again.

'It sure does,' she agreed. 'And if we don't get out of bed right now, we're going to do it all over again.'

'And you'd hate that?'

'No. But I'd probably collapse from malnutrition halfway through. I need food, and I need it quickly.'

'Come on then,' said Mark, and he kissed her and rolled out of bed. He opened the wardrobe and pulled a pair of folded Levi's off a shelf and slid into them. Then he hitched a polo shirt off its hanger and pulled it on over his head. 'I've got the number of Pizza Hut in the other room. Get dressed or I'll change my mind and we'll never eat.'

Katy realised that she was lying naked with her legs apart and her thighs slick and shiny with the detritus of their love-making and blushed. She jumped up quickly and ran past Mark towards her bedroom, where she tugged on her jeans and the check shirt that she'd worn for the journey up to London over her nude body.

'What do you fancy?' Mark called from the living room.

'You,' she said as she walked in to join him.

'Pizzawise.'

'Large Super Supreme with extra cheese and tomato,' she said. 'And a coke.'

'No chance on the coke,' said Mark as he tapped out a number on the phone. 'I've got a bottle of champagne in the fridge. I was saving it for a special occasion, but I didn't know what. Now I do. And when we've drunk that there's some more Chardonnay.'

'Suits me,' said Katy.

Mark ordered two large pizzas and some garlic bread, then together they went into the kitchen where he found two champagne flutes in the cupboard and a bottle of bubbly in the fridge and opened it, not spilling a drop. He filled the glasses and they touched rims and Mark said, 'To us.'

'To us,' echoed Katy.

'But what's going to happen when your parents find out?'

Katy hadn't thought of that. She hadn't thought of much for the last hour or so except for the pleasure that Mark had given to her with his body.

'I don't know,' she said. 'They'll hit the roof probably. If they *do* find out.'

'And hit me a second or two later if your father's anything like I remember him. And they will find out, believe me. People have a way of knowing these things. Especially people with young, beautiful daughters.'

'Don't worry,' said Katy. 'I won't let anyone hurt you.'

'That's not the problem,' said Mark seriously. 'It's just that I'm over twenty years older than you, a trusted relative who's supposed to take care of you on your first solo trip to London, and I end up deflowering you.'

Katy adored the way he'd said 'deflowering you'. She loved to think of her pussy as a flower that Mark had picked at the precise moment when it was ready to bloom.

'People will think I simply took advantage of an innocent young girl at the first opportunity I had. Doesn't sound too good, does it?' He went on.

'Not when you put it like that,' said Katy. 'But that's not what happened, is it?'

'That's how it'll sound,' said Mark, but before he could say any more the pizza arrived.

They ate in bed, and before the pizza and the wine that Mark had brought in from the kitchen was finished, both he and Katy wanted to make love again.

The third time was more leisurely. Mark nuzzled Katy's breasts until they throbbed under the touch of his lips. Katy lay on her back and stroked his hair and felt the heat and need build in her loins. She wanted his cock again. She had never guessed that she would have such a need for sex once she lost her virginity. The insides of her pussy were hungry for his prick. The muscles needed to grasp it tightly and feel his spunk shoot into her again.

He moved his head down her belly, poked his tongue into her naval which made her bite her lip and buck her hips with pleasure, then he moved his mouth further down into the fluff of her pubes and lower still to the lips of her cunt.

She parted her legs and he pushed his nose against her clitoris as he licked out her honey pot. She lay back in the warm room, quiet except for the lapping sounds that Mark was making with his mouth, and she thought that finally she knew what real happiness was, and wished that the feeling of his mouth on her slit could go on forever.

Mark ministered to her sex for five minutes or more, then raised his head and moved up to lay in her arms. She saw that his cock was red and hard between his legs and she put her hand down to stroke his appendage.

'Wank me,' he said, and she did as she was told, gently rubbing the length of his weapon between her fingers. Mark lay very still as she worked his cock up and down. 'I need you,' he whispered.

'I need you too,' she replied.

'Roll over,' he said, and once again she obeyed, and he mounted her from behind, and she opened her legs widely and felt the top of his cock enter her cunt, and he began to fuck her like a dog on a bitch. One hand went to her breasts and he held them both in the palm. She heard him moan and the hot jet of his ejaculation burst between her legs again, and they collapsed onto the bed together. She loved feeling the whole weight of his body on her back.

9

They slept together in Mark's bed with the TV at the foot buzzing away all night. Katy woke at about three-thirty, before it got properly light and lay in the half darkness thinking about all the things she'd done that evening with the man asleep next to her. The more she thought about it, the randier she felt. And after a few minutes, when the need for a cock inside her made her cunt drip like a leaking tap, she put her hand to the still sleeping Mark's groin. His penis was soft and limp, still damp and sweaty from their previous fucks. She played with it for a few minutes and he moaned in his sleep, then she threw back the single sheet that covered them and put her face down to his crotch. His pubic hair was crusted with dried come, and his prick and balls smelled acridly of sex. Katy sucked the whole of his limp dick up into her mouth and she salivated over his skin as she felt his organ start to harden between her lips.

Mark groaned again, louder this time, shifted and woke. He lay for a moment as if wondering where he was and with whom, before saying, 'Katy?'

She let his prick dribble out of her mouth and replied, 'Yes. Who did you expect?'

'You dirty little bitch. Do you want it again?'

'Yes.'

'Carry on doing what you're doing, and you'll get it, I promise.'

She opened her mouth and slid her lips along the length of his cock again, and immediately it grew hard in her mouth, filling it to overflowing.

She grunted herself as she licked the length of his weapon and sucked the sweat and come out of the hair that was matted on his balls.

'That's wonderful,' he said. 'Don't stop.'

Katy had no intention of doing any such thing and she put her fingers into the crack between his buttocks, found his arsehole with the nail of her forefinger and gently opened the orifice until her finger slid in up to the knuckle. It was something she'd never done before, and she wondered how it would affect him.

Mark was in paradise as her nail scratched at the inside of his arse and her mouth moved back to the helmet of his knob. She slid her tongue into the little opening there, making him reach down and catch the thick fall of her blonde hair at the nape of her neck and push her face even deeper into his groin.

After a few more minutes sucking at Mark's cock, Katy was almost choking from the huge hunk of meat that was being forced down her throat, and she pulled her finger out of his bottom and pushed herself away from his body. 'You'll kill me if you're not careful,' she said to Mark. 'I couldn't breathe down there.'

'Sorry, darling,' replied her lover, 'that's the last thing I want to do.'

Katy lay next to him and kissed him on the mouth, their tongues entwined, and as the kiss lengthened

Mark mounted her, their lips still plastered together. Katy found his knob and, by now expertly, slid it into the greased slit between her thighs. He began to move inside her slowly, then said, 'Put your finger in my arse again.'

'Did you like it?' she asked.

'It was wonderful. How did you know about that?'

'I read about it in a book,' said Katy. 'I wondered how it would feel.'

'It felt great to me. Do it again.'

'If you'll do it to me.'

'Of course.'

Katy found his back passage again and gently inserted her finger, then lifted one of her own buttocks to allow Mark's hand admittance into her own crack. It was damp from the juice that had dribbled down it from her pussy, and it took very little pressure from Mark's finger to open the hole and allow his slippery digit entrance.

As his finger slid up the tight wet sheath between the globes of her arse, Katy was in Heaven. She'd played with her own cunt enough until she thought that nothing on earth could give her more pleasure. But the sensation that she felt when Mark's long finger invaded her back passage was the most ecstatic that she'd ever known, and she cried out and came onto his knob straight away.

When Mark heard and felt her release, he began to pump harder at her cunt and within just a few seconds his hot spunk joined her emissions in her cunt.

'That was the best,' he said, as Katy pulled her finger out of his hole, and he withdrew his knob from her pussy and lay next to her.

'You're marvellous,' she whispered into his ear, and as the television set droned on in the background they both fell asleep in each other's arms.

10

Katy and Mark woke again at nine. They lay together in bed and Mark said, 'No regrets?'

'No,' replied Katy with a kiss.

'I thought you might feel differently this morning.'

'No,' she said again.

'Good,' said Mark. 'What are we going to do today?'

'Aren't you working?'

'Not a chance. I'll phone in and tell them I'm working from home.'

'Can you do that?'

'Just watch me.' Then seeing the look on her face, said. 'Don't worry. I often do it.'

'I wouldn't want you to get into trouble on my account.'

'I'm one of the bosses,' said Mark. 'It's one of the few advantages of getting older. A little seniority.'

'Good,' she said. 'So what *shall* we do?'

'Make love, then have breakfast. Get cleaned up, then go out for lunch. And maybe later a little shopping. I'd like to buy you a present.'

'Super,' said Katy.

'What time's your train back home tonight?' asked Mark.

'Oh God, that,' said Katy. 'Do I have to go?'

'No. Hang on for another night by all means. But you'll have to go back sooner or later. You've got to get yourself sorted out to start work next week.'

'And I can still stay here?'

'Of course you can. Don't be silly. You still want to, don't you?'

'Yes.'

'Well, there you go.'

'Can I sleep with you?'

'If you want to.'

'Of course I want to.'

'Every night?' he asked.

She nodded.

'Then you can.'

'Oh good.' She pondered for a moment. 'So what was the first thing we were going to do today?' she asked wickedly.

'I can't remember,' teased Mark.

'Yes, you can.'

'Have a cup of tea?'

'No.'

'Go to the loo?'

'No. Don't tease me.'

'Make love?'

'Yes.'

'So what are we waiting for?' And Mark covered her mouth with his and she felt the rasp of his overnight stubble on the skin of her face.

'I love the feel of that,' she said.

'What?'

'Your beard on my skin.'

'Do you?'

'Yes. Rub it on my tits.'

He did as she said, and put his rough chin down to the tenderness of her breasts and scraped it across her nipples which immediately rose to the occasion.

'You do like that, don't you?' he said, feeling them harden, and he kissed and sucked each hard lump of gristle in turn.

'Mmmm,' she said. 'Do it to my cunt.'

He moved his head even further down her body, and Katy opened her legs as wide as they would go so that she presented as much of the tender wetness of her cunt lips to the roughness of his face as she could, and he gently moved his face around on the damp membrane until she groaned with desire and said, 'Fuck me, please.'

'With pleasure,' said Mark. 'But I want to do it a different way.'

'How?'

'In your arse.'

'Your cock's too big.'

'No,' he whispered. 'I'll show you.'

And with that he rolled her round onto her front and once again using the ooze from her pussy as lubrication, he pushed his finger slowly into her back passage.

The feeling was just as wonderful as it had been the last time he'd done it, but Katy was frightened that Mark's monster dick would split her wide open. However, her fears were groundless. Expertly he opened up her anus with one finger, then inserted a second, then a third until she was bucking up and down on the bedclothes with pleasure. Then he removed his fingers, took a handful of her cunt cream and spread it over the skin of his hard cock, mounted her and inserted his helmet into her arsehole. Katy tensed as she felt his prick enter her.

'Relax,' said Mark. 'This won't hurt, I promise.'

And he was right. The first few seconds when Katy felt invaded by his weapon soon passed, and as he slid his cock centimetre by centimetre down the velvet shaft of her arse, her fear turned to joy and a great warmth filled her body as she accepted his pole into her hole.

When he was in as deeply as he could go and Katy felt the weight of his spunk-filled balls on her bottom, the pubic hair that covered them tickling her skin beautifully, he slowly began to fuck her. As he moved his prick in and out of her arse the feeling of warmth grew even greater and she knew that when she came it would be the most powerful orgasm that she had ever experienced. As her anus opened even wider to his thrusts, he moved faster and faster, and she could hear his breath ripping out of his throat at his exertions. His balls hammered on her buttocks, and Mark put his hand down to her pussy and found her clit with two fingers and pulled the little knob of flesh until with a flare in her breath and a screech from her throat Katy came, pressing her body down hard on the mattress as she did so to gain the maximum pleasure from her release.

Mark kept on fucking her, crashing his body onto her back in a frenzy until he stiffened and called out her name, shooting his load into her backside and filling it with his mighty prick.

11

After Mark rolled off Katy's inert body, she cuddled up close to him and said, 'God, that was great. I never imagined...'

'Did I hurt you?'

'No.'

'Told you.'

'What shall we do now,' said Katy reaching down to Mark's limp and sore penis.

'We'll get up and take a shower,' said Mark, removing her hand. 'Otherwise you'll wear me out.'

'Am I too eager for you?' she asked.

'No. But I'm starved. I've used up so much energy...'

'You poor old man,' said Katy. 'I'll get you some breakfast. Unless you want me to come into the shower with you...'

'Breakfast, I think,' said Mark, rising from the bed and pulling on his bathrobe. 'We can take a bath together later.'

'Is that a promise?'

'Sure is.'

'I'll hold you to it.'

'And I'll hold you to me.'

'Promises, promises.'

He smiled, and left the room, and Katy slowly got up and went and found her robe too, and went into the kitchen and put on the kettle for coffee.

After a leisurely breakfast, they did exactly what Mark had promised. He ran a bath, to which Katy added half a bottle of blue, perfumed bath foam. When the tub was full of hot water with a topping of rich suds they took off their robes and climbed in. The bath was big with mixer taps in the middle, so it was ideal for two, and they lay back in the soft water and looked at each other through the steam that rose from it.

'Happy?' asked Mark.

'Very.'

'Good.' He found her calf under the water and began to massage it.

'You're making me horny again,' said Katy.

'That's the idea.' He moved his foot until his toes were in her pussy, and found her clitoris with his big toe and began to massage it gently.

'That's beautiful,' said Katy.

'Are you wet?'

'Inside?'

He nodded.

'What do you think?' she asked.

'I think you are.'

'You're right.'

Mark's cock began to rise to the occasion, and the knob of it popped out of the water into the foam like the periscope of a submarine.

Katy reached out and began to play with it. 'Feel good?' she said.

Mark nodded in pleasure, and lay further back against the edge of the bath as Katy's hand massaged his prick. 'That feels wonderful,' he said, the sweat rolling down his face and dripping into the bath water.

Katy leaned right forward and took his foamy cock into her mouth. Her hair fell over his belly and trailed in the water, but she didn't care. With expertise she sucked him off. Mark gripped the rim of the bath on both sides and arched his body up into her face. Deeper and deeper she took his cock down her throat, almost choking as it filled her mouth, but reluctant to let one centimetre of the hot meat escape her questing tongue and lips.

She held the hardness of his overflowing balls in one hand and as she felt them jump she sucked hard and collected a mouthful of hit jism for her troubles. She swallowed the warm come, gulping it down her throat as if it was her favourite drink, which in a way it was. When he was spent, she allowed his dick to slip out of her mouth and sat back, licking her lips.

'Tasty?' asked Mark from where he lay, exhausted at the other end of the bath, looking at her through half-closed eyes.

'Delicious.'

'Better than alcohol?'

'Oh much.'

'That's my girl.'

They stayed in the bath for the best part of an hour, washing each other carefully. Katy spent an inordinate amount of time on Mark's genitals, which grew once again under her caresses.

'Do you want it again?' he asked.

Katy nodded.

'You'll wear me out,' he said. 'I must be getting old.'

'Rubbish,' she replied. 'I want you to make me come.'

When Mark was hard again they climbed out of the bath and, still soaking wet, fucked on the bathroom carpet. Mark slid up inside Katy's slick cunt, and she gripped his cock tightly with her thighs as he pumped in her on the floor. Katy came twice before Mark wailed and shot his load into her again.

They lay locked together in the humid atmosphere of the bathroom and Katy stroked Mark's sweating back as he regained his breath.

'You're an animal,' he said. 'I never realised.'

'I just like fucking,' replied Katy. 'It's the most fun I've ever had.'

12

Katy phoned through to her mother and told her that Mark had taken the day off to show her around town, and that she was going to stay another night and return home first thing the next morning. Katy's mother agreed that it was a good idea, and told her to enjoy herself. Katy replied that she'd make sure that she would.

Then she got dressed. She put on her sexy black undies with sheer nylons and suspenders, the flower-pattered dress she had brought with her especially for that day, did her make-up and presented herself for Mark's approval.

'You look wonderful,' he said. 'Beautiful and summery.'

'But underneath,' she said, pulling up her skirt to show off her black knickers and suspender belt, 'I'm dark and interesting.'

'So you are,' said Mark. 'And if you want that lunch and the present I promised you, you'd better pull down your frock, or we'll never get out of here today.'

'What a lovely idea,' said Katy. But she dropped her skirt nevertheless, and they went out together into the warm summer air and caught a cab up to the West End.

They lunched in a ludicrously expensive Chinese restaurant in North Audley Street, where the waitresses wore long silk dresses split up both sides almost to the waist, and there seemed to be a waiter for every diner present. Then after coffee and liqueurs, Mark walked Katy down to Bond Street where he bought her a beautiful enamelled bracelet that perfectly matched the colour of her eyes.

'It's beautiful,' said Katy, admiring her new acquisition, when they were seated in a nearby hotel that served afternoon tea. 'This has been the best day of my life.'

'It's not over yet,' said Mark. 'But you'd better not tell your mum and dad that I bought it for you. They might smell a rat.'

'Our secret then,' said Katy conspiratorially.

After tea they cabbed back to Waterloo where Mark bought a bottle of wine at the off licence on the corner of his street.

'Let's go home for a while,' he said. 'Then later we can go to the Italian restaurant for a farewell dinner.'

'You're spoiling me,' said Katy.

'That's what I'm here for,' he replied.

They went back to the flat and Mark opened the wine while Katy waited for him in the living room. She sat on the sofa and opened the top two buttons of her dress so that the cups of her bra were exposed, and crossed her legs, pulling her skirt up above her stocking tops. When Mark entered the room carrying two glasses of wine he smiled at the sight of her and asked, 'Are you trying to tell me something?'

'Do you need telling?' Katy asked back.

He handed her a glass, sat next to her and put his hand on the tops of her naked thighs. 'Not really.'

'I'm going home tomorrow.'

'Sadly.'

'But I'll be back at the weekend.'

'Happily.'

'I don't want you to forget me.'

'As if I could.'

'I want to leave you with as many happy memories as possible.'

'You have.'

'But I want to give you more.'

Mark smiled. 'That's good.'

'And I want a few more of my own.'

'Whatever you want.'

'Then take off my panties and stick your tongue up my cunt. I want you to make me come again.'

Mark uncrossed her legs for her, and did as she said, gently removing the tiny lace and net garment that covered her pearl of womanhood, and put his face down to her fragrant minge, inhaled the perfume of her lust and kissed her hairy puss.

Katy hooked her legs over his shoulders and closed her thighs, trapping his head into the delta of her maidenhead, and Mark licked and sucked at the softness of her snatch until she almost swooned with pleasure, and came in a series of hard jerks against his mouth.

Mark sucked out her sweet juices and swallowed them down, much as Katy had swallowed his in the bath that morning. As she lay back, totally relaxed, he took his head away from her cunt and drank a mouthful of wine. 'You were right,' he said, 'it does taste better than alcohol.'

Katy stood up and, in a burlesque of a stripper routine, undid the rest of the buttons of her dress and slowly pulled it off, letting it drop to the floor. Then bumping and grinding with her naked hips, she undid her bra and let first one, then the other strap slip off her shoulders before dropping it to the floor too, allowing her breasts full freedom. Still gyrating her body, she came right up to the sofa where Mark was sitting and shoved her cunt right up to his face again. 'Do you want me to leave my stockings on?' she whispered.

He nodded, and she sat on his lap and they kissed deeply. As their mouths plastered together, his hand roamed over her almost naked body, delving deep between her legs where her cunt was still hot and wet from his earlier ministrations. She opened her thighs wide and he slid her off his lap onto the sofa, then got up and started to tear his clothes off.

'You're horny too,' said Katy.

'You bet your life,' replied Mark, as he removed his underpants and stood before her, his prick engorged with blood, and his balls hanging full and heavy between his legs.

'Come here and give that beautiful thing to me,' said Katy, and Mark did just as she said.

He joined her on the sofa, and they began to kiss again. Mark covered Katy's face with his lips, wetting her skin with his saliva and biting at her lips and tongue, then moving down to her neck and naked breasts, where her nipples were hard, hot and

71

rough under the softness of the inside of his mouth.

Katy arched her back towards him as he petted her tits with his mouth, and she moaned deeply in her throat and reached for his prick, which she massaged gently between her fingers.

At that, Mark ran his hands over her belly and down to her pubic hair where he found her slit, open and waiting for his fingers. He felt her clitoris as hard as a pea under the pads of his fingers, and tweaked it gently, causing Katy to moan louder and search out his mouth with hers again. Her lips were soft on his and she drew his tongue into her mouth where she chewed at it with her teeth and licked it with her own tongue.

Mark gently laid her back on the cushions of the sofa, mounted her, and slid his stiff prick up into her waiting tunnel of love in one smooth motion. She gasped as she felt his rod of meat invade her tight little cunt and force it open with the power of his love.

'Fuck me,' she cried. 'Fuck me hard, darling. I need your spunk inside me.'

Mark didn't need to be told twice. He shoved his cock up inside her willing quim, and felt it grow even harder as the wet silkiness of her pussy gripped it tightly.

Katy crossed her legs around Mark's back and rubbed the nylon of her stockings across his skin, and the feel and sound of the sheer material rasping up his spine drove him to fresh frenzies of fucking.

Mark pushed inside Katy's cunt as deeply as he could go, until the knob of his cock was up inside her womb and the feeling of the engorged flesh deep inside her most intimate parts tore an orgasm from her body. One orgasm followed by another, and yet another until the sweat poured off Katy's body and she gouged long scratches out of Mark's shoulders with her sharp fingernails.

Ecstatic with the effect his love making was having on the teenage girl squashed between his body and the sofa, Mark yelled with pleasure and poured the contents of his balls into her welcoming body. A long, hot eruption of love juice that made her come for the fourth time.

Totally spent, he fell on top of her and as his prick softened and popped out from between the lips of her cunt, they lay together, bonded by sweat and the sweet glue of love, gently caressing each other's bodies until they fell asleep.

13

Mark woke up about an hour later. He was lying awkwardly across Katy's prone body. He stretched and yawned, looked at the clock and gently disentangled himself from her long, smooth limbs and stood up. He rescued his underpants from the floor where he'd dropped them, and hopped from one foot to the other as he put them on.

He gently shook the sleeping girl's shoulder and her eyes popped open. 'Hi, sleepyhead,' he said. 'Getting hungry?'

Katy nodded, stretched too, showing her almost naked body to its best advantage as she did so, and said, 'What time is it?'

'Nearly seven. Want to go out?'

Katy nodded again and Mark rescued her dress and passed it to her. She stood up and gracefully slipped into the garment and fastened the buttons.

'No knickers?' he asked.

She shook her head this time. 'No,' she replied. 'I want to feel our come run down my legs. And no bra either. I've never gone out before with nothing on but stockings and suspenders. Do you think anyone will know?'

'If they do, they'll be very jealous of me being with you.'

'Then I hope they do,' said Katy.

'You're disgraceful,' said Mark.

'I was a good girl till I met you. Or at least, not a bad girl,' she said.

'Sez you.'

'That's right. Sez me. Now give me five minutes to put on some make-up and comb my hair, and I'll be ready.'

Mark put on the rest of his discarded clothes as Katy went to the bedroom to find her hair brush, and finished his glass of wine whilst he waited.

By the time she returned to the living room, looking stunning and not the least like she'd recently been fucked for the second time that day, Mark had rescued the bottle from the kitchen.

'You look beautiful,' he said. 'Have some wine.'

'So do you. And yes I will,' said Katy.

They sat close together on the sofa and toasted each other and their happiness before going out for the short walk to the restaurant.

They got an intimate, candle-lit table for two at the back of the restaurant, and Mark ordered a bottle of Chianti straight away.

'If I have much more wine to drink today, I'll be tiddley,' said Katy.

'And uninhibited?' said Mark.

'You mean you think I'm inhibited now?' asked Katy, 'Sitting here with you, wearing no bra or knickers and my bottom all wet and squidgy with come.'

Mark laughed out loud, 'I've never met anyone less so. You're the least inhibited girl I've ever met.'

'And the wine will make me worse,' said Katy.

'I don't see how it could.'

'Just wait till we get home and I'll show you,' she said with a wicked grin.

'Do I have to? We could get under the table and do it right here.'

Katy giggled. 'Don't make me laugh,' she said. 'Every time I do, more dribbles out. The back of my dress is soaking.'

'Not a dry seat in the house,' said Mark.

Katy giggled again, then said. 'I told you not to. You're making me leak again. I'll have to go to the loo and dry myself off.'

'I wish I could come with you.'

'You're awful,' said Katy, getting up from her seat. 'You dare follow me and I'll complain to the manager and he'll have you arrested.'

'A night in the cells would be worth it.'

'A night with me would be better.' And she blew him a kiss, and with a twitch of her lovely bottom was gone.

After a leisurely dinner, they walked slowly back to Mark's flat, arm in arm. It was a lovely summer evening and the warmth in the air remained long after darkness fell.

Mark poured two brandies when they were alone again in his living room and they drank deeply.

'This has been the most marvellous weekend of my life,' said Katy. 'Thanks to you.'

'Mine too,' said Mark. 'Thanks to you, my love.'

'I'm going to hate to leave tomorrow.'

'Don't think about it. We've still got tonight.'

Katy blushed slightly. 'Yes we have, haven't we.'

'When are you coming back?'

'I thought Saturday.'

'Good idea. That'll give us the weekend together before you start work.'

'It'll be lovely.'

'As lovely as you,' said Mark, putting down his glass on the table, taking Katy's from her, placing it next to his, then taking her in his arms.

She looked up into his face and they kissed. A long, deep kiss which excited Mark so much that his prick grew and pushed into the softness of Katy's belly. She leant against him and the feel of his cock made her cunt weep in anticipation of what was soon going to be filling it.

'You're hard,' she whispered.

'And you're soft,' Mark whispered back, as he ran his hands over her body, almost totally free of underwear under the thin material of her dress.

'Bed,' she said.

'Good idea.' And he picked her up in his strong arms and carried her off to the bedroom.

Mark placed Katy carefully on her feet beside the bed and she kicked off her shoes and started to unbutton her dress. He watched as she gracefully took off the garment and draped it over a chair, then stood boldly in front of him, dressed only in her suspender belt and nylons, her breasts standing proudly, nipples hard and erect. She touched herself between her thighs and pulled a face. 'It's dried all sticky,' she said. 'And look at my stockings.'

Mark looked at where their mutual come had dried to a hard crust on the darker bands of material at the tops of her nylons.

'Take them off for me,' she said.

He knelt on the carpet before her and nuzzled his face between her legs and smelled the stale sex that lingered there and felt himself aroused at the odour.

He gently unfastened the four suspenders that held up her stockings, and rolled them down her legs and off her feet. Then when she turned in front of him, unhooked the suspender belt and threw it over her dress.

'Shall I have a shower first?' she asked, when he stood again.

'Afterwards,' he said. 'I want you now.'

'I guessed you would,' she said, looking down at the bulge clearly visible in his trousers. 'I want you too.'

Katy lolled on the top of the bed, and watched as Mark stripped off again in front of her. She loved the muscular shape of his body, and the way his cock jumped up when it was freed from the restriction of his underpants, and allowed herself to feast her eyes on the hard sacks of his balls, covered in dark pubic hairs, which hung down between his legs. When he was naked he joined her on the bed.

'I want to taste our sex again,' he said, between kisses.

'Drink at my fountain,' she whispered. 'And I'll drink at yours.'

They moved around until Mark's head was at her groin, and her's at his, and they began to lick each other.

Katy's cunt was hot and wet and Mark couldn't get enough of it, and he pushed his face deep into her cleft as she took his cock in her mouth and tasted their residue on it too.

They sucked and licked each other, the sound of

their lapping filling the room. And as Katy's fresh lubricant dribbled from between her legs, Mark drank it down deeply.

After a few minutes Katy took his cock out of her mouth and pulled him up next to her so that they could kiss again and suck their juices off each other's lips. Without a word, Mark mounted his teenage lover and his cock slid easily into her waiting snatch and they began to fuck wildly.

They slammed together in a frenzy until Mark felt his sperm rising.

'I'm going to come,' he cried.

'Wait for me.'

'I can't.'

'I'm not ready.'

'I can't stop it.'

'Stick your finger up my arse then.'

Mark moved his hand under Katy's writhing buttocks. The crack between her cheeks was warm and sticky and he found her arsehole and inserted his forefinger, and pushed it up her dark passage.

'Christ, yes,' she screamed. 'That's it. Spunk me, darling. I want it. I'm ready too.'

Mark could hold himself back no more and with a gush he filled her cavern with his jism, pushed his finger up her backside even harder, and at the first rush of his liquid sex Katy pulled him close and covered his cock with her own orgasm.

14

The next morning, Mark was up before Katy was awake and roused her with a cup of tea.

'You're up,' she said. 'And not up me. That's a shame.'

'I have to go to work,' he replied. 'If I stayed in bed with you I wouldn't get in till lunchtime.'

'That wouldn't matter. You're one of the bosses aren't you? Come back in to bed and drink this tea with me.'

'No,' said Mark firmly. 'I'm going to get dressed and go and earn a crust.'

'You cruel beast.'

Mark hesitated, then shook his head and said, 'You little temptress. I'm not going to fall for that one.'

Katy pouted prettily, then said, 'Alright, Mark. But I warn you, you'd better get ready for a very sexy weekend when I come back.'

'I'll lay in a dozen bottles of baby oil for the occasion.'

He went into the bathroom, returned and put on business clothes whilst Katy teased him with her body from where she was lying. She played with her breasts, moaning as she pulled them up and kissed them, teasing her nipples until they were red and hard, and finally put her hand inside her cunt and played with her clitoris until she came noisily. When she had serviced herself, she licked her fingers. 'That tastes sooooo *good*,' she said, then wriggled her fingers at her lover. 'Want to try some?' she asked wickedly.

'You're a filthy little beast,' said Mark. 'I've got to go to the tube with a hard on. I'll have to wear a coat or I'll get arrested for some obscene crime or other.'

'Come over here and I'll give you some relief,' offered Katy.

'No,' said Mark. 'For the last time. I'm going to be late as it is.'

He went over to kiss Katy goodbye, and she tried to wrestle him into bed, but he fought her off bravely, and almost ran to the bedroom door to escape, although they both knew that he didn't want to. 'You're insatiable,' he said from the doorway. 'I'll see you on Saturday.'

'I'll phone you before then,' replied Katy. 'From my bedroom, and I'll tell you exactly what I'm wearing, and what I'm doing.'

Mark shook his head in mock reproof, blew her a kiss and left.

Katy stayed in bed for another half hour or so and masturbated again before getting up, taking a shower, getting dressed in jeans and a shirt, packing her case and leaving the flat, locking it up securely behind her.

She caught a mid-morning train and was home by early afternoon.

Katy's mother was indoors, and congratulated her daughter warmly on getting the job she had wanted so much.

'When are you going back?' she asked.

'Saturday.'

'We're all going to miss you. Especially your father.'

'And I'll miss you too. But London's only a couple of hours away. I'll come back often, and you can come up and visit me.'

'Of course we will. By the way, Dave called,' said Mrs Dunn. 'I told him your news. I don't think he was best pleased.'

'He'll get used to it,' said Katy.

'He's going to call later. He wants to see you.'

Katy shrugged. 'I think it's all over, Mum,' she said.

'Well, at least tell him to his face.'

'I will.'

The phone rang at five. It was Dave.

'I hear you got your job,' he said.

'That's right,' said Katy.

'Well done,' he said. Although Katy knew it took an effort for him to say it. 'When are you going to move up to London?'

'On Saturday.'

'Oh.'

'I start work on Monday.'

'So soon.'

'Yes.'

'Can I see you before you go?'

'Of course.'

'Tonight?'

'I'm tired, Dave. I fancy an early night.'

'Tomorrow then?'

She knew that she was going to have to face him sooner or later. 'OK,' she said.

'I'll call for you.'

'Fine.'

'What time?' he asked.

'Seven.'

The doorbell of the Dunns' house rang at seven precisely the next evening. Katy was waiting in the living room alone watching TV. She was as horny as hell and missing Mark rotten. For her last date with Dave she was wearing a denim skirt and a plain white blouse over Marks and Sparks cotton underwear. On her bare feet she wore a pair of low-heeled white shoes. She was devoid of make-up. She didn't want Dave to get the wrong idea about their meeting, but still she was aroused. She'd had so much sex over the past weekend that her body couldn't get used to the idea that she wasn't going to get any more for another few days.

As she stood up from the chair where she was sitting to answer the door, she felt the crotch of her knickers wet with desire and even the thought of going out with Dave made her tummy flutter.

He was standing inside the porch holding a bunch of flowers when she opened the door.

'For you,' he said, thrusting them into her hand.

Katy was rather taken aback. In all the time she'd known him, he'd only bought her flowers once. On the occasion of her last birthday.

'Thanks, Dave,' she said awkwardly as she accepted the gift. 'Do you want to come in?'

'No,' he replied.

'Well I'll just pop these into water.' She turned and hurried into the kitchen, grabbed an empty vase off a shelf, splashed water into it, unwrapped the flowers and dropped them in.

Her mother was standing by the sink.

'Dave brought them,' Katy explained. 'I don't know why.'

'I do,' said her mother. 'Leave them. I'll arrange them for you in a minute.'

'Thanks, Mum,' said Katy. 'I'd better dash. He won't come in.'

The two women looked at each other as if to say 'Men', and Katy hurried back to the front door.

Dave was standing on the front path and she joined him. She gave him a swift peck on the cheek and said. 'Thanks, Dave. The flowers are lovely.'

He shrugged. 'Want a drink?' he asked.

'Sure.'

'The car's outside.'

They went out to his Capri, and Dave pointed the car towards their favourite pub. A small, friendly place on the outskirts of town.

They said little on the journey. Dave put on a tape of The Police, and turned up the volume. Katy was glad of the distraction, but even so the short journey seemed to take an age. She could smell Dave's aftershave, and his own masculine smell beneath that, and although she didn't want to be, she couldn't help being turned on by it.

Dave parked the car and they went into the pub where he ordered a pint of lager for himself and a half for Katy. When he'd been served he brought the drinks over to the table in the corner where she was seated.

He took a sip from his drink and said, 'You don't seem too pleased to see me.'

'Oh Dave,' said Katy. 'I'm sorry. It's just that I'm tired and there's so much to do . . .'

'Before you leave,' he finished her sentence for her.

'That's right.'

'And go to London.'

'You know I've always wanted to.'

'And leave me behind.'

She leaned over and touched his hand. 'I'm sorry,' she said.

'You'll meet someone else.' His voice rose with emotion.

Katy felt suddenly guilty. 'Maybe,' she said.

'Definitely. We're finished aren't we, Katy?'

'We can still be friends.'

'I don't want to be *friends*.'

'I'm sorry,' she said again.

'Finish your drink and we'll get out of here.' His voice rose some more.

'I haven't started it yet.'

That seemed to calm him down a bit, and they drank in silence, but Katy's lager seemed to stick in her throat.

When she'd finished her drink, she said. 'I think you'd better take me home now.'

Dave nodded, and finished his pint in one long swallow, then stood up and they went out of the pub together, back to the car. Dave started it up and he wheeled it out of the car park.

Katy was still feeling horny, and sorry for the way things had gone with Dave, and as she glanced out of the corner of her eye at him, she realised that she quite fancied him. Or she quite fancied the idea of having sex with him as a way of saying goodbye.

'Park up,' she said, and her voice sounded husky in her own ears.

'What?'

'Park up. I want to talk to you.'

'I thought you'd said everything.'

'Dave. Just park.'

He did as she said, and turned the Capri off the main road and ran it up a slight hill into a deserted clearing with a view of Bristol dead ahead that they often used for their snogging sessions.

Tonight, thought Katy, now fully aroused, there'll be more than snogging going on.

As soon as Dave turned off the engine and killed the lights Katy leaned over, pulled his face round and kissed him. 'I'm sorry, darling,' she said. 'But let's not quarrel. Let's make tonight one to remember.'

She could see that Dave hardly believed his ears at what she was saying, but he kissed her back strongly and ran his hands down over her breasts and felt the hard nipples through her shirt and the thin cotton bra beneath.

'What do you want?' he asked.

I would have thought that it was obvious, thought Katy. After all this time of wanting to get inside my knickers, I give you the green light and you don't know what to do.

'I want you to fuck me,' she said.

She saw Dave's eyes widen in the reflected lights from the city beneath them.

'What, now?' he said.

'Now.'

He began to unbutton her shirt, and his hands felt hot when they touched her bare skin, and she felt her cunt open in anticipation of his knob. She put her hand down to his groin and felt it rise beneath the touch of her fingers within the denim of his jeans.

'Are you sure?' he whispered.

'Quite sure. I want you, Dave. Don't you want me?'

'Of course.'

'Then do it. I need you badly.'

Dave finished unbuttoning her shirt, tugged it out of the waistband of her skirt and pushed it over her shoulders. He tugged it off and threw it into the back seat of the car, then pushed her bra up over her breasts without undoing it and put his mouth down to her nipples. He licked and sucked at them, pulling them with his lips until they were rock hard and hurting.

Katy began to tug at his clothes too, and with his help he was soon naked to the waist, and she found *his* nipples with her greedy little mouth and sucked and bit at them until he cried out, half with pleasure, half with pain.

'Get naked,' she said. 'I want to be naked with you.'

Dave kicked off his shoes, pulled off his socks and struggled out of his tight jeans and underpants, allowing his cock the freedom it needed and it stood proud between his legs pointing at the roof of the car.

Katy unhooked her bra, wriggled out of her skirt and pushed her panties down over her hips to join her skirt in the well on the passenger side of the car. She fumbled with the controls of the seat and said. 'How do I get this to go back.'

Dave leaned over her and his chest squashed her breasts as he worked the lever that reclined the passenger seat until it was almost horizontal.

'Climb on me, Dave,' she whispered urgently. 'I want your cock inside my cunt.'

Still hardly believing his ears, Dave did as Katy said. He manoeuvred himself on top of her, and without any foreplay she found his cock and worked the knob of it into the wet, open slit between her legs.

Dave pushed himself in as far as he could go and started to grind his groin against hers.

To Katy, the feeling of being fucked was wonderful, and she pushed her lips up to meet his as his prick worked at the inside of her cunt making waves of pleasure run through her body from head to toe.

They kissed passionately, and once again, Katy felt a momentary pang of guilt. This time that she was betraying Mark, but her body was crying out for satisfaction and she ignored the feeling as she pushed harder at Dave's body.

The car shook as they fucked, and sweat boiled off their bodies and mixed in a slimey froth as they banged against each other in the close confines of the car.

Katy locked her legs behind Dave's back to keep his cock firmly inside her soaking cunt, and he screwed her harder as she pulled him closer to her hot body.

'I'm going to come,' he shouted.

'Do it, baby,' she called back as she felt her body start to tell her she was ready for orgasm. 'Do it to me. Shoot me hard.'

Her words goaded him to fuck her harder, and as he did so, she felt his balls jump between the cheeks of her arse, and a jet of boiling spunk erupted inside her pussy. As he orgasmed, she squeezed his cock tightly with her cunt muscles, and came herself with a great hot flush of relief.

Katy lay back as Dave slumped on top of her. His body felt like it weighed a ton, but she didn't mind playing squash with him and the knobbly material of the car seat. Jism oozed out of her cunt and trickled down her thighs as he shifted position, and when his cock softened she felt it slip out of her cunt.

They lay like that for a few minutes before Katy said, 'Shift off, Dave, my legs are going to sleep.'

As he moved over the gearstick and slumped in the driver's seat, Katy felt their sweat cool as it dried on her skin.

'You weren't a virgin, were you?' he said after a moment.

Katy shook her head. She could feel him looking at her in the dimness inside the car.

'Did you meet someone in London?'

She nodded.

'Who?'

'Just someone.'

'You didn't waste much time.'

'It just happened.'

'Why didn't you tell me?'

'I don't know.'

'You used me.'

'I thought you wanted to make love.'

'That wasn't love. That was lust.'

Katy shrugged. She was beginning to learn that there wasn't much difference when you boiled it down.

'Were you thinking of him when we did it?'

'No.'

'I don't believe you.'

'Believe what you like,' said Katy. She was getting tired of Dave. He was just a baby, and she longed to be with a real man.

She started to get dressed, and Dave found his clothes and tugged them on.

'I'll take you home,' he said.

'Fine.'

They were both silent throughout the journey.

When he dropped Katy off outside her house, he drove off without a word.

And you never even kissed me after, she thought, as she watched the tail lights of his car vanish up the road.

15

Katy went back London on the first train after breakfast, Saturday morning. Mark met her at the station and they caught a cab back to Waterloo and made love straight away.

Katy had put on new, sexy lingerie that morning, under a dark blue, button-fronted dress with a long skirt, but by the time they reached Mark's flat her knickers were soaked. They hardly dared touch in the cab, knowing that they would be unable to control themselves once they started. But as soon as the flat door was closed behind them, Mark dropped her bags on the floor and they were on each other like a dog and a bitch suddenly released from behind barbed wire.

They kissed madly, running their hands over each other's bodies and Mark pulled Katy's full skirt up to her waist and pushed his hands under the elastic of her tight knickers and found the sopping mess of pubic hair between her legs.

She pushed herself on his hand, almost orgasming right there and then in the hall, and put her fingers to his groin and felt the hardness of his prick beneath the soft material of the khaki chinos he was wearing.

91

'I want you,' Katy said unnecessarily.

Mark pulled her panties to her knees, knelt in front of her and fastened his mouth to her cunt. Her juices tasted heavenly, and he swallowed mouthfuls as she shoved her mound against his face and gripped his hair in both of her hands.

Mark pulled her down next to him and ripped open the buttons of her dress and tore off her bra to free her breasts for their mutual pleasure. He licked at the smooth skin of them and sucked the nipples up into his mouth and chewed at their hardness until Katy almost fainted with pleasure.

'I want you,' she said again. 'I've missed you so much.'

Mark left her lying on the floor, her dress open and her knickers still around her knees, as he tore off his clothes and climbed on to her soft body and kissed her mouth as she found his knob with her fingers and guided it into her love tunnel, and they were one again.

They moved together in a sweating frenzy, their mouths plastered together and their hands roaming over each other's bodies, squeezing and stroking as their ardour grew, and Katy split the material of her new knickers as she forced her legs apart to allow him easier access to the centre of her.

Mark concentrated hard on not coming. His balls felt as hard as unripe apples as they bounced up and down on the curves of Katy's bottom. Ever since she'd left on the previous Tuesday, he'd been dreaming of the moment when they coupled again, and he didn't want to spoil it by ejaculating prematurely. But the girl was so passionate, and the sensation that he felt as she rubbed the length of her cunt on his cock made it hard for him to stop himself shooting his wad into her.

'Slow down, Katy,' he panted. 'Make it last.'

'I want to come.'

'Wait!' he ordered, and pulled himself out of her whilst he could still control himself.

'Don't go,' she cried, lying on her back on the carpet, her dress spread out around her, her make-up smeared across her face, naked apart from that and the thin suspender belt and dark nylons she was wearing.

To Mark, she looked about twelve years old. A little girl who'd been deprived of her favourite toy. The fact that her favourite toy was about ten inches of hot cock was immaterial.

'Have patience,' he said, pulling his chinos over his nakedness. 'It's all right for you. I take a little time to get ready again.'

'Poor old man,' she said. 'I'll make you ready in a minute.'

'The spirit is willing, my dear girl. But unfortunately, the ageing flesh is weak.'

Katy smiled from where she lay. 'I think you're the greatest. Ageing or not.'

'You're so kind,' said Mark. 'Let's have a drink before I take you to bed to finish the job.' And he reached down, gave her his hand and pulled her to her feet.

'OK,' she said. 'You big tease. But when you're ready again, I might not be.'

Mark swatted at her bottom and she ran into the kitchen buttoning herself up as she went.

Katy opened the fridge and pulled out a bottle of white wine that was cooling there, got down a couple of glasses from the cupboard and watched as Mark uncorked the bottle.

'You're a bloody tease,' said Katy as her cousin filled the two glasses to the brim.

'Plenty of time,' he said. 'I thought we'd get some lunch first.'

'*Before!*' she wailed.

'Yes. You young people have got to learn to wait for your pleasures.'

'Mark.'

'Hush,' he said. 'Drink your wine.'

'Oh you.' But Katy smiled as she said it. Her whole body was vibrating with need, but she knew that the prolonged waiting would only make the satisfaction to come more complete.

Katy went to the bathroom, washed her face, re-did her make-up and got changed from the skin outwards, and she and Mark headed for their favourite Italian restaurant, where they were greeted like old friends and shown to a quiet table in a corner, shielded from the other diners by a number of ferns and cheese plants in huge earthenware pots. Mark ordered a bottle of Chianti whilst they perused the menus.

'Hungry?' he asked, when the wine had been served.

'For your cock,' replied Katy.

'Now stop that. And be serious.'

'I am.'

He smiled at her and touched her hand with his. 'You're very sweet, Katy,' he said. 'And very rude.'

'But you like me.'

'Of course I do. I more than like you. You know that.'

Katy smiled and found his leg with her foot and ran it up his calf. 'I'm soaking again,' she said. 'Thank goodness I didn't put any knickers on.'

'Sshh,' said Mark. 'Someone will hear you.'

'I hope *someone* does,' she said. 'One of the waiters is really dishy. I wouldn't mind him showing me where he keeps his salami.'

'You're disgusting.'

'Well, if you think more of your stomach than you do of my ... er ... nether regions. Then a girl has to do what a girl has to do. And talking of stomachs,' she said, picking up a bread stick, peeling the cellophane off it, putting a knob of butter right on the end and nibbling it off in a most suggestive way, 'I'll have the vegetable lasagne with a green salad on the side.'

'I see that what's going on in your ... er ... nether regions as you put it hasn't exactly interfered with your other appetites. I'll get the waiter over.'

'Make sure it's the one I fancy,' said Katy, and dissolved into gales of laughter.

After lunch they rushed straight back to the flat and went to bed.

Their love-making was urgent at first. They tore off their clothes and went naked into each other's arms, falling onto the duvet together as they kissed and caressed. Mark was hard as soon as he saw Katy's naked form, made all the easier by the fact that she was wearing nothing but stockings and a suspender belt under her dress. And she was still aroused from their previous love session.

This time he didn't enter her until, by kissing her breasts and playing with her clitoris, he made her come, and then she lay back and welcomed his cock into her sopping cunt, and Mark only had to pump her a few times before he shot his load into her waiting womb.

PART TWO

16

The first time that Katy saw Sir Charles Wheeler was late on the Tuesday evening of her second week in the typing pool at the oil company. She'd settled into the routine of her job well and was thoroughly enjoying her new found independence at work, and her sex life with Mark at home. Her immediate boss, Lucy Sawyer, who had interviewed her and, in fact, was the same woman who had offered her the job, seemed to like Katy and another of the typing pool, a young married woman called Daphne Richardson, had taken Katy under her wing and they were fast becoming firm friends.

Katy was just getting ready to go home that evening and was alone in the typing pool when Sir Charles burst through the door carrying a slim brown folder in one hand.

Katy had no idea who the distinguished-looking fifty-something with a full head of greying hair and matching moustache, wearing a beautifully cut double-breasted suit, white shirt, striped tie and highly polished black shoes was. But one thing was certain. He was important.

'Where's Mrs Sawyer?' he demanded.

'I'm afraid she's gone home,' said Katy.

'Damn,' he said, looking at the solid gold watch on his wrist. 'I didn't realise it was so late. Who are you?'

'Katy Dunn,' said Katy, resisting the impulse to curtsy as she did so.

'Can you type?'

'Yes.'

'My secretary's off sick. I need this report typed yesterday. Do it for me will you.'

'I was just going home.'

'Miss Dunn, you are an employee of this company. I am a director. This report is urgent. It's less than three pages long. If you are any good at your job you will finish it in fifteen minutes. Now will you do it?'

Katy put down her bag and took the folder that Sir Charles was holding and opened it. Inside were three pages of neat handwriting. His, she presumed.

'Do you want it laid out like this?' she asked.

'Exactly like that.'

'Fifteen minutes,' she said.

He turned on his heel and walked out of the room again. 'I'll be back,' he said.

Katy sat down and turned on her word processor. 'Please,' she said to the empty room, 'thank you.'

In fact the report took Katy slightly longer than she'd expected, and Sir Charles had returned just as she was laying out the final paragraphs. When she was satisfied she put the computer in its 'print' mode and ran off a copy.

Sir Charles grabbed it, read it, nodded, and asked for another five copies.

Katy ran them off, and Sir Charles put them into the folder with his original manuscript and walked out of the room without another word.

'Good night to you too,' said Katy to the door as it closed behind his retreating back.

And she still didn't know who he was, although she was soon going to find out.

The next morning when Katy arrived for work, Lucy Sawyer called her into her office.

'Good morning, Katy,' she said. 'I believe you did some work for Sir Charles Wheeler last night after everyone else had gone home.'

'I did some work for someone,' replied Katy. 'I don't know who he was. But he said he was a director, and he was very rude. He didn't even say thank you.'

'That was Sir Charles,' said Lucy. 'He was very pleased with what you did, although you probably wouldn't know it. Congratulations. Thanks for saving the day. His secretary is on extended sick leave and the man doesn't know what to do without her. We can't find a replacement who comes up to his high standards, and he's making a total nuisance of himself . . . But don't say I said that.'

'I won't,' said Katy.

'Anyway. Thanks again. You're going to do well here, Katy, with your sort of attitude.'

Katy smiled, and after one or two more pleasantries went back to her desk where Daphne was waiting, looking very pretty in a tight pink sweater and a black mini skirt.

'What was all that about?' she asked.

Katy told her what had happened and what Lucy had said. 'I wish it had been me. I think he's a dish.'

'He's a bit old isn't he?' asked Katy.

'Not too old for me,' said Daphne with a grin.

'Especially if what I hear about him is true.'

Before she could explain, the morning's work was delivered and she ran back to her desk.

17

Katy thought about what Daphne had said about Sir Charles Wheeler as the week passed, and decided that her friend was probably right. He was dishy, for an older man. But then she dismissed him from her thoughts until on the Friday morning, once again she was summoned into Lucy Sawyer's office upon her arrival at work.

'Katy,' said Lucy. 'Sit down.'

Katy did as she was told. What's up? she wondered. Have I done something wrong?

'Don't look so worried,' said Lucy, 'I've got some good news for you.'

Katy looked mystified.

'You remember that job you did for Sir Charles Wheeler?' asked Katy's boss when the younger woman was seated in front of her desk.

Katy nodded.

'And you also remember that I told you his secretary was on extended sick leave?'

Katy nodded again.

'Well, it turns out that it's nothing too serious, but she's not likely to be back for a while, what with convalescence and everything else.'

Katy nodded for a third time, wondering what that had to do with her.

'And the upshot is,' Lucy continued, 'that Sir Charles needs a temporary secretary, and he was so impressed with the way you stayed late the other evening, and the quality of your work, that he's asked for you.'

Katy was thunderstruck. 'B-b-but I'm not a secretary,' she stammered. 'And I've only been here a couple of weeks.'

'It makes no difference to Sir Charles. He wants you as his secretary's stand-in, and Sir Charles generally gets what he wants in this organisation. You start in his office on Monday at nine-thirty sharp.' Lucy said firmly. Then when she saw Katy's expression her tone softened. 'Don't worry, Katy,' she continued, 'it's nothing that you can't handle. Any problems, come and see me. Sir Charles's staff handle most of the day to day business. It happens like that when you become a director of a company this size. All you'll have to do is a few memos and reports like the one on Tuesday, and answer the phone. That won't be a problem, will it?'

Katy shook her head. She couldn't believe what was happening.

'Your salary will be adjusted to mirror your new position during your time upstairs,' said Lucy. 'And if you do well, you'll be snapped up by one of Sir Charles's executives. That's generally what happens. So you'll probably never come back into the pool at all. You're a very lucky young woman.'

'Thank you,' said Katy. But she still wasn't sure.

'It's a pleasure. Now go back to your desk and finish your tasks for today. And good luck on Monday. Sir

Charles's office is on the thirteenth floor. Suite one-oh-five. You're moving up in the world, and you deserve it.'

Katy left Lucy Sawyer's office in a daze. Daphne noticed her friend's condition and came over to her desk. 'What happened?' she asked. 'You look like you've been hit by lightning.'

Briefly, Katy told Daphne about her conversation with Lucy Sawyer, and her elevation to the position of Sir Charles Wheeler's temporary secretary.

'Crikey,' said Daphne. 'You must have impressed the old boy. Look we can't talk now. Are we on for lunch as usual?'

Katy nodded.

'See you at one then, you lucky thing.' And Daphne went back to her own desk.

As one o'clock struck from Big Ben, Daphne and Katy went upstairs to the staff canteen with its view of the City of London. When they had selected their food, they took their trays to an empty table at the far side of the restaurant.

'You'll be too grand to eat here soon,' said Daphne when they were seated.

'How do you mean?' asked Katy.

'You'll be eating in the management restaurant after next Monday.'

'I'm not management,' protested Katy.

'You are as Sir Charles's secretary,' said her friend. 'No more mixing with us mere mortals.'

'I'll still come and have lunch with you.'

'No, you won't. If we meet, it'll have to be outside. It's all round the office already. The other girls are dead jealous.'

'I don't know why. It's only temporary. Till his

secretary comes back from sick leave.'

'It's not only being Sir Charles's secretary that they're jealous of.'

'What then?'

'Oh Katy, you are innocent.'

Katy sat with a forkful of food halfway to her mouth and looked puzzled. 'What are you talking about?' she asked.

Daphne looked around to make sure no one could overhear and leant closer to Katy. 'Sir Charles doesn't just choose his secretaries for how fast they are at shorthand.'

'What then?' said Katy, obviously still at a loss.

'He chooses the girls that he fancies, you silly goose. He always screws them. It's well known.'

Katy replaced her fork on her plate and felt a faint vibration above her nylons at her friend's words. 'Are you serious?' she asked.

'Course I am.'

'I didn't know.'

'You soon will. I'm jealous too.'

'Are you?'

'Course I am. He's gorgeous. I'd love to take some *dick*-tation from him.' She emphasised the first syllable of the word, even though it was quite clear what she meant.

'Daphne, you're a married woman.'

'What difference does that make?'

'You shouldn't talk about other men like that.'

'Why not?'

'Because you shouldn't.'

'You can tell you've never been married,' said

106

Daphne. 'Talking about other men is the only thing that keeps me sane.'

'You're mad,' said Katy.

Daphne raised her eyebrows and said, 'Tell me that when you've been married as long as I have. Anyway, we're talking about Sir Charles. Don't you think he's a doll?'

'Not bad I suppose. But I still think he's a bit old.'

'Experienced, I call it. He makes me wet.'

Katy knew what she meant. She was beginning to experience a warm seepage into her knickers herself, just talking about her new boss.

'Daphne, you're terrible.' she said, as she rubbed the tops of her thighs together under the table. 'But what happens if his secretaries don't fancy *him*?'

'Then they don't last very long. *That's* what happens. Why? Don't *you*?'

'I don't know. I've never thought about it.'

'Liar,' said Daphne, and smiled. 'I bet you have.'

'Well, maybe a bit,' said Katy, and she reddened.

'I can tell you have,' said Daphne. 'Look at you, you're blushing.'

'I am not.'

Daphne didn't reply, instead just pulled a face. 'Well, do you?' she asked after a moment.

'A bit maybe,' said Katy.

'There, I told you so. I bet he gets your knickers off within a fortnight.'

'*Daphne*,' said Katy. 'Don't be so rude.' But the seepage into her knickers was turning into a flood, and her nipples had hardened inside her bra cups at the thought of Sir Charles removing her most intimate garments.

'He could get my panties off anytime,' said Daphne. 'I bet he's got a lovely cock.'

'What would your husband do if he heard you saying things like that?' said Katy.

'He'd probably ask if he could watch,' replied Daphne. 'Will you promise to tell me what happens when you're all alone with Sir Charles up in that office?'

'Of course,' said Katy. 'But I bet he doesn't do anything.'

'How much?'

'How much what?'

'How much do you bet?'

Katy was astonished. 'Are you serious?' she said.

'Of course. How much?'

'I can't.'

'Course you can. Come on. How about a bottle of champagne?'

'Alright then. But I'm sure you'll lose. He doesn't fancy me.'

'Oh yes, he does. I've heard all about that crafty old devil. I'll tell you what. Two bottles says that he tries it on before next Friday. But you must tell the truth.'

'Course I will.' said Katy. 'And two bottles it is.'

18

When Katy got home after work, Mark was already in the flat preparing dinner.

'You're home early,' she said.

'I got bored with work. Then thought POETS.'

'POETS?' said Katy, mystified.

'Piss Of Early, Tomorrow's Saturday.'

'You're mad,' she said and kissed him.

'So what's new?' he asked, as he twisted the cork out of a bottle of cold white wine and filled two glasses.

'Loads,' said Katy, and told him her news, but not including Daphne's story, or their bet.

'Exciting stuff,' said Mark, and raised his glass in a toast.

It is, she thought. I wonder if Sir Charles really does fancy me, or if Daphne's just saying that to tease me.

On Monday morning, after Mark had left for work, Katy washed her hair, applied her make-up just a little more thickly than usual, and dressed carefully for her first day as Sir Charles Wheeler's temporary secretary. Remembering what Daphne had said, and even though she wasn't actually convinced, she wore her tiniest black silk panties; their net insert in the front allowed her curly pubes to poke through cheekily, and at the back they were cut high across the cheeks of her bottom and exposed most of her buttocks. The matching bra was low cut and underwired to push her already pert breasts up and apart. The black suspender belt with tiny bows covering the front stocking fasteners completed the set, and she pulled her sheer, dark stockings up tightly and checked that the seams were straight in the mirror in the spare bedroom. She put on a black silk blouse and noted that if she undid the second button, her cleavage looked magnificent. I'll remember that, she thought as she did the blouse up to the top. She put on the skirt of her new black suit and checked that there was no visible panty line. Thank goodness for silk undies, she thought, but did notice that as she walked the fastenings of her suspenders were clearly outlined against the smooth material. So what? she thought, but her cunt dampened at the thought of Sir Charles noticing, and realising that she was wearing stockings, not tights. She quite liked the thought of a powerful man like that finding her attractive, and even if he didn't, so what? No one would know except her about the special attention she'd paid to her lingerie.

Finally, she put on the suit jacket and stepped into shiny black leather court shoes. She took one last look in the mirror, thoroughly approving of what she saw, picked up her handbag and left the flat.

19

Katy took the lift to the thirteenth floor, and found
suite one hundred and five by nine-twenty. She stood
outside the imposing door, then plucked up her cour-
age and opened it, entered, and found herself in a
large office with a huge window overlooking the river.
There was a desk with a word processor centred upon
it, a paper shredder to one side, and three telephones
lined up neatly. One red, one white, one black, next
to an intercom. This she assumed to be her work-
station. There was a set of double doors, which she
assumed led into Sir Charles's inner sanctum, opposite
the suite door itself. In one corner of the room there
was a miniature kitchen, complete with a drip filter
coffee machine, a jar of coffee beans and a grinder.
Someone had put a carton of fresh milk in the tiny
fridge next to the sink. Next to that was a door that
led into a small cloakroom, and then another beyond
it that led into a lavatory, complete with wash basin.

My own loo, thought Katy. How grand.

She shut the door to the cloakroom and went over
to the set of double doors.

I wonder if he's in, she thought, then knocked once
and entered. Inside was an office easily twice as big as

her own, with another panoramic view of the Thames through a massive picture window, a huge polished desk empty except for one white phone and behind which sat a leather executive chair. A matching sofa at least twelve feet long backed up against the window behind a long, black coffee table. The office was deserted. There was a further door in the far wall, and Katy knocked again before opening it. Inside was a full-sized bathroom with a round bath, a shower stall, wash basin and toilet. It, too, was empty, and Katy stood in the doorway and looked round. Crikey! she thought. This is bigger than the one we've got back home. The way some people live! She went back into her office, and, in the absence of anything else to do, decided to brew a pot of coffee, which she did right away. She took a cup over to her desk and sat down.

Sir Charles Wheeler strode into the office at nine forty-five precisely. He was wearing a charcoal grey suit, with a crisp white shirt, a striped silk tie and black shoes, buffed to a high shine. There was a folded copy of *The Financial Times* under one of his arms. Katy stood up as he walked in the room. 'Sit down,' he ordered firmly, waving her down with his right hand. 'You don't have to stand up for me.'

Katy felt those now familiar vibrations above her stocking tops at the sight of him, and she shivered as her pussy involuntarily opened and a drizzle of rich, warm lubricant began to wet the tight crotch of her silk knickers. God, she thought, Daphne was right. He *is* a dish, and I *do* fancy him.

Sir Charles stopped in the doorway that led into his office. 'Coffee, please Miss Dunn. White with one lump of sugar. Then give me fifteen minutes and we'll start work.' And he went inside and closed the doors firmly behind him.

No 'Good Morning.' No 'How are you?' No 'Well done for getting the coffee brewed.' And no 'Please' when he asked for it. Ordered it really, thought Katy, as she poured out Sir Charles's coffee. Miserable old sod. But somehow the offhand way he treated her made him more attractive, and she licked her lips and rubbed the tops of her naked thighs together. God, she thought, I wonder if Daphne was having me on about him fucking his secretaries. I hope she wasn't.

She took the coffee through and placed it on Sir Charles's desk. He didn't acknowledge her until she was at the door. 'Shut it on your way out,' he said.

Katy did as she was told and got another coffee for herself and went back to her own desk, wishing she'd remembered to bring a daily paper of her own.

Ten minutes later the intercom on her desk buzzed. She pushed down the 'Listen' button and Sir Charles said: 'Come in, Miss Dunn. And bring a shorthand pad.'

Katy did as he said and went into Sir Charles's office. He was sitting behind the desk with *The Financial Times* open in front of him.

'Good morning,' he said with a smile. 'I'm afraid I'm a bit of a bear until I've had my first cup of coffee.'

Katy was a bit taken aback by his change of attitude.

'And welcome. I'm glad to have you here. My secretary, Miss Campbell, is sick as you know. I'm afraid she made herself quite indispensable to me. I hope you'll do the same.'

Katy nodded.

'I'm sorry I haven't been able to speak to you personally before this, about coming in as my temp. But I was away at the end of last week and I telephoned Mrs Sawyer late on Thursday after you'd gone.'

'That's alright,' said Katy. 'It was just a bit of a surprise. I didn't think you were too pleased with me the first time we met.'

'Life is full of them, surprises, that is. And quite the contrary. I was most taken with your attitude. Staying late and all. It's just that I was preoccupied at the time. Anyway, I hope you have a good time working up here. It's a bit of an improvement over the typing pool I should imagine.'

Katy looked round. 'Yes, it is,' she agreed.

'Good. Shall we get down to work then?'

'Of course.'

'Actually,' said Sir Charles, echoing Lucy Sawyer's words. 'I'm a bit of a fake really. I've got such good staff backing me up that I hardly have a thing to do these days. It was different once . . .' he paused, 'but then you don't want to hear the memoirs of an old man, do you?'

'I don't mind,' said Katy. 'And I don't think you're old at all,' and she blushed.

'Another time perhaps. And thank you. But for now, I've got two short memos for you to type, and I'm afraid that's it for the day. All you have to do is sit in the other room, answer the phone and tell me if anyone important dies.'

Katy looked amazed.

'Joke,' said Sir Charles.

Katy smiled. Thank goodness, she thought.

'Will you sit on the sofa, or do you want to bring in your chair from your office?' asked her new boss.

'I don't mind.'

'You sit on the sofa then, and I'll pace.'

Katy walked over to the long leather chair and perched on the edge, but she kept slipping back on the shiny hide and she felt her skirt ride up her thighs.

'Make yourself comfortable,' said Sir Charles as he rose from his chair and crossed the thick carpet to stand over her.

'Yes, Sir Charles,' said Katy, and allowed herself to slide back on the rich material of the sofa. Her skirt rode up to the tops of her stockings and she pulled it down, but she knew that Sir Charles had noticed by the gleam in his eye.

'Are you ready?' he asked.

For anything, thought the young girl as she looked up at the powerful man looming over her. Goodness, I think he *does* fancy me. Daphne was right. I wonder if I'm going to lose that bet we made.

'Yes, Sir Charles,' she said, opened her shorthand pad and crossed her legs which sent her skirt sliding up the smooth material of her nylons again. She saw Sir Charles's eyes move to the hem of her skirt as she tugged it down self-consciously, aware that the fastenings of her suspenders could be clearly seen through the material. What the hell, she thought.

The two memos that Sir Charles had to write were short, and within ten minutes his dictation was over.

'That's it,' he said. 'If you'll get those typed, I'll sign them.'

'What else is there to do?' asked Katy.

'Not much. Just answer the phone. Not that it rings

115

often. All calls for me go through to my staff office downstairs, and they know I never take calls until eleven.'

How strange, thought Katy.

'Just one other thing,' said Sir Charles.

'Yes?'

'It's rather personal. I hope you don't mind.'

'No.' Be as personal as you like, thought Katy.

'Do you wear stockings, Miss Dunn?' Sir Charles asked.

Kate blushed crimson. '*Sir Charles*,' she said.

'I thought you didn't mind me being personal.'

'I don't.'

'Then do you?'

'Yes, Sir Charles,' she said.

'Are you wearing stockings today?'

'Yes, Sir Charles.' Although she was sure he knew.

'I hope that my asking you has caused no offense, but you must realise that as my secretary, by definition, we are going to be on quite intimate terms.'

'I don't mind, Sir Charles.' Katy could feel her cunt turning to water. Intimate terms, she thought. The terms couldn't be intimate enough for her.

'What are you doing for lunch?'

Katy was taken aback by the change of subject. 'Nothing in particular,' she said.

'Then I'd like to take you out and buy you a present. To welcome you onto the team as it were.'

'There's no need . . .'

'Of course there is, and afterwards we'll have lunch. I'll have a car ready for twelve-thirty. Now if you'll just type up those memos . . .'

Katy went back into her office with her mind in a turmoil. She was now certain that her attractive, sexy, middle-aged boss did fancy her, and she wished that she could talk to Daphne about it. But of course she couldn't see her friend at lunchtime as she now had a date with Sir Charles. Even the thought made her weak at the knees. Never mind, she thought. What will be, will be, and she switched on the word processor on her desk and got down to work.

As Big Ben struck the half hour at twelve-thirty, Katy and Sir Charles descended in the directors' express lift from the thirteenth floor to the garage in the basement. Sir Charles's Jaguar waited there with his chauffeur, whom he introduced as Hartley, at the wheel. They were driven to Harrods, where Katy was very aware of the charisma of the man sitting on the leather seat next to her as they chatted, and Sir Charles instructed his driver to wait. 'We won't be long, Hartley,' he said. 'Then it's back to the office, via that rather fine restaurant in Archer Street. I'm sure Frederick will be able to squeeze us in.'

'Very good, sir,' said Hartley, before he jumped out of the car and opened the back door to allow Katy to leave the car, closely followed by her handsome boss, whose eyes she was sure lingered on her long legs and the flash of bare thigh that she exposed as she climbed out of the low-slung limousine.

They went straight up to the lingerie department, and Katy could hardly believe her ears when Sir Charles started discussing the various styles, colours and materials of underwear with the assistant, who seemed to know him well.

'What do you think of these, Miss Dunn?' he said eventually, holding up a pair of very brief, white silk lace panties and matching half bra.

'They're lovely,' replied Katy, blushing under the gaze of the assistant.

'Do they have a matching suspender belt?' asked Sir Charles.

'Yes, sir,' said the assistant.

'What colours do you have them in?'

'A full range. White, black, strawberry, lemon, petrol blue, navy blue and grey.'

'I'll have a set of each. Put them on my account. The young lady will give you her sizes – Miss Dunn?'

Blushing again, Katy reeled off her vital statistics, then turned to Sir Charles as the assistant gathered the various garments together. 'You shouldn't,' she said. 'I'm sure they're far too expensive.'

'Not at all,' said Sir Charles in reply. 'My staff are entitled to nothing but the best.'

'But so many colours . . .'

'Nonsense,' said Sir Charles. 'One for every day of the week. Now, don't worry your pretty little head, Miss Dunn. It's all taken care of. I've got more money than I know what to do with, if that's the problem. And I like to see my secretaries well turned out.'

He wants to see them, thought Katy, and her tummy turned over at the thought. Well, if that's what you want, that's what you shall get. But I shall make you work for it, you saucy old devil.

When the transaction was finished, and Katy was presented with a bulging Harrods bag full of her new undies, Sir Charles signed a chit for the bill which, when the assistant totted it up, made Katy's head spin.

Sir Charles took her arm and led her back to the car and the waiting Hartley, who drove them to a small, but very chic, restaurant in Archer Street. There, she and Sir Charles were greeted like royalty and led to a discreet table at the rear of the restaurant that Hartley must have booked by telephone from the company Jaguar whilst the shopping expedition had been taking place.

Frederick, the head waiter, had a dry martini waiting by each place setting, and Sir Charles said, 'I hope I wasn't presumptuous, ordering these. You do like martinis I hope.'

'I don't know,' said Katy truthfully. 'I've never had one before.'

'My dear girl,' said Sir Charles, 'it is so refreshing to meet someone like you. I envy you your youth, and to have so many new things to try.'

Not as many as a few weeks ago, thought Katy, but enough. She tried her drink. It almost brought tears to her eyes it was so strong, but gave her a delicious warm feeling in her stomach after a moment or two.

Sir Charles took total control of the lunch. He ordered the food and wine for both of them, and Katy allowed herself to dip her toe for the first time into the world of privilege and money, which she had never experienced before. Soon she realised she liked it very much.

20

When Katy got back to the flat that night, she hid her new underwear under some sweaters in the chest in her old room. She didn't want Mark asking awkward questions about where they'd come from. She'd gradually start to wear them, and tell him that she'd gone on a spending spree with her credit card in anticipation of her first month's wages, especially as she had already been awarded one pay rise on her promotion to the position of Sir Charles's temporary secretary.

Sir Charles. Even the thought of him was starting to give her collywobbles. And the more she was with him, the more she desired to be held and loved by him. God, she mused, and to think I considered him too old. He's perfect.

As she was thinking about Sir Charles, she heard Mark's key in the door, and guiltily she went to greet him.

'Hello, sweetheart,' he said. 'How was your first day in your new job?'

'Lovely,' replied Katy. 'Not that there was much to do.'

'There never is when you get as far up inside an organisation as he has,' said Mark. 'The atmosphere's too rarefied. But was he alright to you?'

Perfect, thought Katy. 'Couldn't have been better,' she said.

'Good. So what's to eat?'

'I had a big lunch. I'm not very hungry.'

'OK. I'll knock something up for myself out of the freezer. Then maybe we'll take a bottle of wine to bed.'

Katy, who had been feeling horny all day, couldn't think of a better idea.

And when, an hour later, she and Mark were lying naked together on the bottom sheet of the bed, with the top sheet and duvet tossed aside, all she could think of was Sir Charles Wheeler. Katy closed her eyes as she kissed Mark and pretended that it was her boss's lips that covered hers, his tongue that entwined with her tongue, and that it was his teeth that nibbled at the fullness of her bottom lip. If only Mark had a moustache, thought Katy as their mouths mashed against each other. It would be perfect. She'd never kissed a man with a moustache before, and was eagerly looking forward to the experience. I wonder what it would feel like if he kissed my breasts, thought Katy, and then my cunt. What would his hairy top lip feel like on my hairy minge? And how lovely it would be to lick my juices off it afterwards. Her cunt flooded at the thought, and when Mark put his hand down to it he said, 'You're soaking.'

'You're turning me on,' said Katy.

'I'm flattered,' said her cousin.

If only you knew, thought Katy, and closed her legs on his probing fingers and wished that it was Sir Charles's hand that was rubbing her clitoris and making her cunt weep for a hard cock.

Katy was particularly passionate that evening. Her body was on fire as Mark fingered her pussy and kissed her breasts, bringing the nipples up like two hard, hot stones that he licked and kissed until she could hardly bear the feeling, they were so tender and sensitive. She reached for his cock and began to wank the foreskin over the swollen head of it, and closed her eyes again and dreamed that it was Sir Charles's cock she was playing with, and what it would feel like inside her, and what kind of lover would he be. She imagined him to be hard and cruel, but with a tender, loving side to his nature, much as he was at work. I want Sir Charles to ride me, she thought as Mark mounted her, and she felt his helmet sliding between the sopping lips of her cunt. I want him to fuck me, she thought as Mark began to push his cock in and out of her, and she held him closely as she responded to his movements with movements of her own. I want him to shag me, she thought as she felt his meaty rod sliding up and down the soft, moist skin inside her pussy, and his balls banged against the crack of her arse. I want his spunk inside me, she thought as Mark's movements became faster and his strokes shorter. I want him to fill me with his juice, she thought as she felt Mark stiffen over her, and his fingers dug into her back, and he shot his load deeply in to her womb. I want to come on his lovely prick, she thought, as she felt the heat of her own orgasm burn through her belly and she tightened the muscles of her cunt on Mark's penis and cried out with pleasure as she came too. I want him to crush me with his body, she thought as Mark slumped down on top of her, and his cock softened and slid out from her slit. And I want to feel our honey drip out of me, she thought, as the warm mix of Mark's jism and her lubrication ran out of her cunt and down between her buttocks and soaked into the sheet beneath her.

21

The next morning Katy decided to wear a set of her new underwear for work. Sir Charles did buy it for me after all, she thought. And it'll make me feel horny wearing it, and I can tell him how it feels, and maybe even let him take a peek. She got quite hot at the very idea, and had to mop her wet pussy with a tissue before she put on her new undies. She chose the black set. She knew how good she looked in black lingerie, and how it contrasted with the peaches and cream colour of her body, and made the skin of her thighs between stocking tops and knickers look milky white by comparison.

The lingerie had been expensive, but Katy decided it had been worth every penny when she'd put it on. It fitted perfectly, made her shapely figure look even more desirable, and was like gossamer to wear.

She was in her office by nine-thirty and had the coffee brewed when Sir Charles came in at nine forty-five. He looked gorgeous in a beautifully cut, double-breasted grey suit, and he stopped, sniffed the air and nodded approvingly when he arrived. 'Very good,' he said. 'Bring me in a cup, and we'll start dictation at ten.'

'Yes, Sir Charles,' said Katy meekly, got up from her chair, poured him a cup, followed him into his office and placed it next to his newspaper and left, closing the door behind her.

At ten precisely she took her pad and pencil into his office.

'Right, Miss Dunn,' he said. 'If you'd like to get comfortable, we've just got a couple of things to get through this morning.'

Katy sat down on the leather sofa and slid back, and felt the hem of her navy blue skirt she'd worn that morning head northwards up the smooth material of her nylons. Sir Charles got up from his chair and walked over towards her. This time he made no secret that he was looking up her skirt, and she in her part made no attempt at pulling it down, instead crossed her legs and felt the slippery hide that covered the sofa cool on her bare thighs at the back, and knew that from where he was standing Sir Charles could probably see the whiteness of them, but she didn't care.

His eyes greedily devoured the sight and Katy fancied that she could see his cock harden in the soft wool of his well-cut suit trousers. He coughed and cleared his throat and asked Katy to take a letter to the managing director of a chain of service stations that sold the company's oil products.

About halfway through the letter, he stopped and said, 'Miss Dunn, are you wearing the lingerie I bought you yesterday?'

Katy blushed, although she was half expecting the question. 'Yes, Sir Charles,' she whispered. She wanted to act coy and innocent for the older man, an act that she thought would drive him mad with desire for her youthful body.

'Do you like them?'

'They're beautiful.'

'They're the correct size?'

'Perfect.'

'Good. Will you model them for me?'

'*Sir Charles.*' Katy blushed even deeper. She couldn't help it, although she knew that sooner or later he had to ask. Once again she acted the innocent, lowering her head and peering upwards through her thick eyelashes. 'I can't. What would happen if someone came in?'

'No one will.'

'But what happens if someone comes into my office looking for me?'

'They won't. Everyone in the building knows not to disturb me or my secretary before eleven.'

'What happens if the phone rings?'

'It won't. But even if it did, you'd answer it like the perfect secretary that you are.'

Dressed just in bra and panties, suspenders, stockings and high heels, thought Katy. That would be lovely. But she wasn't going to agree to anything without teasing him a little first. 'What do you want to see?' Although she knew perfectly well, and the knowledge was making her randier than she could ever remember being in her life; her cunt open and dribbling her juice into the gusset of her new silk panties.

'Everything,' said Sir Charles. 'I want to see what I bought you yesterday.'

'What do you want me to do?'

Sir Charles smiled. 'Pull up your skirt. Let me see your stocking tops.' And he went back to his chair and sat down.

Katy did as he said. She stood up and slowly pulled up the hem of her skirt, to reveal more of her nylon-clad thighs, then the darker band of nylon at the top of her stockings, the fastenings and finally the naked flesh at the top of her thighs and the black straps of her suspenders.

Sir Charles relaxed back into his seat and smiled. 'You have lovely legs, Miss Dunn. Quite superb.'

Katy blushed again. 'Thank you, Sir Charles,' she said softly. She loved feeling his eyes on her legs and wanted to show him more. Everything, in fact.

'Now show me your panties,' said Sir Charles. His voice was hoarse, and Katy realised the effect she was having on the handsome man. She looked at his crotch and she could clearly see the shape of his knob beneath the expensive material of his trousers. Oh God, she thought, I want to hold it, caress it, kiss it, suck it, wank it, and most of all fuck it until it gives me his lovely spunk.

Katy hiked her skirt up higher, pulling it above the brief black knickers and matching suspender belt that she was wearing.

Looking down at Sir Charles's groin again, she saw that his prick was fully hard and poked through his trousers at her. From where she was standing it looked huge and powerful, and she almost swooned with desire for it.

'Do you want to see the bra?' she asked.

Sir Charles nodded, and Katy undid the buttons on her blouse and revealed her lace-clad breasts.

'Do you like them?' she asked.

Sir Charles nodded again. Katy took off her blouse and unzipped her skirt, letting it drop to the floor and daintily stepping out of it. She turned slowly for her audience of one, then walked up and down in front of Sir Charles's desk, his eyes followed her every move. She was so wet between her legs that she knew that her knickers must be soaked through as if she had wet herself, but she didn't care.

'Do you like them?' she asked. 'Are they as pretty as you thought they'd be?'

'Very much so,' he said. 'But I think we'd better go back to the dictation.'

Oh, you cruel man, she thought. Now it's *you* that's teasing me. 'Do you want me to get dressed again?'

'It would be more proper.'

Bastard, thought Katy, as she quickly pulled on her blouse, but left the front half unbuttoned, and slid into her skirt. 'You can sit on my lap while we do it,' said Sir Charles. 'Lorraine always did.' Lorraine was Sir Charles's last secretary.

'Did she?' said Katy. 'Then I'd better too.' And she walked over to Sir Charles's chair and sat down on his lap. It was the first time that she'd been so close to him and she could smell the tang of his expensive cologne; it filled her head like a drug. She could feel his hard cock pushing into her bottom and she moved her buttocks until it slid into her crack. She opened her pad and sat with her pen poised over the pages as if it were an everyday occurrence, which she sincerely hoped that it would be. As Sir Charles finished dictating the letter she could feel his cock get harder and hotter through their clothes, and her cunt leaked

128

into her panties even more as Sir Charles's right hand caressed her bottom and his left rested on the tops of her thighs. Katy felt as if she were in Heaven.

22

When the dictation was over, Katy leant back against Sir Charles's chest and looked up at him. If ever a girl wanted to be kissed and caressed it was she. She wanted to hold him and to be held back. But instead he patted her on the bottom in a businesslike way and said, 'To work, Miss Dunn. I have an early luncheon appointment and I want those letters out of the way.'

Reluctantly Katy got up from his lap and went back to her office. She was angry and confused. Was he just teasing her again? Or had she done something wrong? Perhaps she wasn't pretty enough, she thought. But that was silly, if what Daphne had said about him fancying her was true. And he'd obviously liked the way she looked in her new lingerie.

She sat in front of her word processor, then picked up the phone, dialled the number of the typing pool and asked to speak to her friend.

When Daphne came on the line, Katy asked her if she was free for lunch. She wanted to talk to the older girl, tell her what had happened and ask for her opinion. She knew that she could trust Daphne, and that she'd be dying to hear about what had happened between Katy and Sir Charles.

They agreed to meet in a nearby pub at one, and after she had hung up the receiver, Katy transcribed the dictation and took it back for Sir Charles's signature.

He signed the letters with no reference to what had occurred earlier. In fact his attitude was rather cold and distant, and when he left for lunch at noon, he barely acknowledged Katy's existence, which only made her hornier than over, and she pulled a face at his retreating back as he left the office.

At one o'clock Katy entered the pub and saw Daphne standing at the bar ordering a drink. 'Hi, Katy,' she said. 'What do you want?'

A good fuck, thought Katy, but said, 'Half of lager.'

'Anything to eat?'

'Maybe later. Or I might take something back. I'm not very hungry.' Not for food at least, she thought.

The two girls took their drinks over to an empty table in the corner. 'So what's up?' said Daphne. 'How are you getting on with Charlie Wheeler?'

Katy told her.

When she had finished, Daphne said, 'The dirty old bugger.'

'Not dirty enough,' said Katy. 'I was dying for it this morning. He could have done anything. Anything at all.'

'Don't,' said Daphne. 'You're making me feel randy, and Bob's away all week.' Bob was Daphne's husband.

'Where?' asked Katy.

'A conference. There's always something. I'm sure he's got another woman.'

'*Daphne!*' said Katy.

The older girl shrugged. 'Well it looks like you lost the bet.'

'He hasn't done anything yet,' said Katy gloomily.

'He's bought you seven sets of silk undies, had you parading around in black lingerie in front of him, and given you dictation with his hand up your skirt. All in less than two days. I'd hardly call that nothing.'

'But he hasn't done what I want him to do. He hasn't even kissed me.'

'He will. He's just making you wait. He probably wants you begging for it. You lost the bet, Katy. Now pay up like a sport.'

'Alright,' said Katy, with a grin at her friend's reassuring words. 'When?'

'Friday. Bob's not back till Saturday lunchtime, so we can have some fun. There's a new pub opened by Bennett's Wharf, just down the road. It's supposed to be wild on Friday nights. Loads of dishy blokes get in there.'

'What would Bob say if he found out?'

'Let me worry about Bob,' said Daphne. 'I know how to get round him.' And she winked wickedly. 'Are you on for it?'

'Suits me,' said Katy.

'You'd better wear some of your new undies in case we pull. And you can tell me all the fresh developments between you and Charlie boy.'

'I doubt that there'll be any.'

'I bet there are,' said Daphne, but this time Katy declined to take the bet on.

23

When Katy got back from lunch, there was a message waiting for her to say that Sir Charles would not be back that afternoon. With nothing much to do, she sat in her office until six reading a paperback book she found in one of her desk drawers. She had no visitors and the telephone didn't ring.

When she got home she was preoccupied, and barely touched her supper. After the meal, Mark asked, 'What's the matter, darling?'

'Nothing,' lied Katy. 'Just work, you know.'

'Is your new boss driving you too hard?'

Katy had to smile, despite herself. 'Hardly,' she said. 'No, it's nothing. Just the new job.'

'You'll get used to it,' said Mark.

'I expect I will,' replied Katy. 'I think I'll go to bed now, I'm tired.'

So she did.

The next morning she dressed in her best black two-piece suit again, over a white blouse, the new white underwear Sir Charles had bought her and dark stockings. She carefully made up her face before leaving for work, but looked ruefully in the bathroom mirror and thought, what's the point?

She arrived at her desk on time and made the coffee. Sir Charles swept in at nine forty-five as usual, except that on this occasion he was casually dressed and carrying a gym bag. Katy took him his cup, and placed it next to his open copy of *The Financial Times* as she had done every morning that week.

'Very good,' he said. 'Dictation at ten?'

Katy nodded and left the room. This is getting boring, she thought.

But not for long.

When she returned to Sir Charles's office carrying her notebook and pencil, he stood up as she entered, and said, 'I've been playing squash this morning. I need a shower. Come in and scrub my back.'

Katy was thunderstruck. And even more so, when her boss began to remove his clothes. She watched open-mouthed as he took off his shirt, revealing a muscular chest covered with a mat of grey hair. Then kicked off his shoes, pulled off his socks, unzipped the khaki pants he was wearing and lowered them to reveal a pair of pale blue boxer shorts already tented with an erection.

'Sir Charles,' said Katy, who couldn't help staring at his groin. 'Are you sure you should be doing this?'

'Of course I am,' he replied, and pulled down his shorts and stood naked before his teenage secretary.

Sir Charles's was only the fourth cock that Katy had ever seen in the flesh, and it was by far the biggest. It was enormous. A beautiful love rod that she knew would rule her forever. It was long, hard and veined, and stuck out proudly from the tangle of grey pubic hair that covered his massive bollocks. He was hung like a prize bull, and Katy could only guess at the amount of spunk that those huge balls contained. But one thing was certain. She wanted to find out.

'Come on, girl,' said Sir Charles. 'Get your clothes off. You can't get into the shower, all dressed up like that.'

'Sir Charles,' said Katy. 'I can't.'

'Of course you can. You're my secretary.'

'But that doesn't mean that I'm your property.'

'Yes it does.'

Katy had never been so excited. Her cunt was weeping, and her tits felt as hard and heavy as grapefruit inside her bra.

'Oh, Sir Charles,' said Katy. 'What if someone comes in?'

'No one ever comes in here without an appointment. You know that. They know that it would be more than their jobs are worth. And it'll be more than your job is worth if you don't do as you're told.'

'You're ordering me to undress?' she asked, with a quiver in her voice.

'That's right. You didn't mind posing for me in your lingerie, or sitting around with your skirt up to your crotch while taking dictation.'

'That was different, Sir Charles. Secretaries are supposed to do that. And you did buy me those beautiful undies. But stripping naked, and showering with you . . .'

Sir Charles smiled. 'You know you want to.'

Katy smiled back. Of course she did. But she wanted to tease him again. 'What about my hair? It'll get soaked.'

'There's a hair drier in the cupboard in the bathroom.'

It seemed as if he had an answer to everything. 'Alright,' she agreed. 'But I want to keep my knickers on.'

'What colour are they?'

'White.'

'White silk?'

'Yes. The ones you bought me.'

Sir Charles smiled again. 'Alright I'll allow that. Now go into the bathroom and get ready, and I'll be with you in a jiffy.'

Katy walked into the bathroom and started to undress. What would Daphne think of this? she wondered as she kicked off her shoes, took off her blouse and skirt, hung them on the hook behind the bathroom door, unfastened her bra, shrugged out of it and added it to the rest, undid her stockings and rolled first one then the other off her legs. Katy smiled to herself. She'd probably think that I was the luckiest girl in the world. Finally Katy unhooked her suspender belt, and tossed it over the rest of her clothes.

Seconds later Sir Charles entered. He looked approvingly at Katy's figure and she felt her nipples harden under his gaze. She covered her breasts with her hands.

'You're a good looking filly, Miss Dunn,' he said. 'Don't cover up your best assets,' and he slapped her hard on her left buttock. The slap felt like a kiss to Katy, and she moved her hands to expose her tits to his eyes once again.

They stood facing each other. Sir Charles totally naked and Katy wearing just her brief white silk panties.

'In you get, girl,' he said.

Katy was nearly fainting with desire as they stepped into the shower stall together, as Sir Charles switched on the water and it began to beat down on them. Within a second Katy's white silk knickers were transparent, and Sir Charles made no secret of the fact that he was enjoying seeing her triangle of blonde pubes, clearly visible through the thin material.

'Turn 'round,' he ordered, and Katy did as he said, and she could feel his eyes devouring the sight of the crack between her buttocks.

'Now wash me, girl,' he said. 'Every part of me.' Katy turned around again to face him, took the soap from its dish and held it under the water and made a rich lather between the palms of her hands.

She started soaping Sir Charles's chest, and as she moved in close to him, the knob of his cock pushed against her belly.

'Wash my John Thomas,' ordered her boss.

Trembling, Katy took his huge member in her hands, and it stiffened even more at her touch and seemed to grow another inch in length.

'It's so big,' she said. 'I can't get one hand round it.'

'It is a beauty, isn't it?' said Sir Charles proudly.

'And I bet you know how to use it.'

'It has seen some use,' he said. 'And women tell me that I know what to do with it.'

'Have you had a lot of women?'

'Hundreds.'

'Your other secretaries?'

'Of course. That's what you're there for, isn't it?'

'To please you?'

'Yes.'

'And do I?'

'What?'

'Please you,' said Katy, as she soaped Sir Charles's cock and felt it grow even harder under the tender ministrations she was giving it.

'Yes,' replied Sir Charles, as he leant back against the tiles inside the shower stall and pulled Katy close for a long, lingering kiss. Their first. What Katy had been waiting for all week. And it was worth the wait. His mouth was soft and warm on hers, and she loved the feel of his moustache on her face.

The warm water beat down on their naked bodies as they stood embracing each other, their mouths glued together, and Sir Charles's huge cock squashed between their bellies. The kiss seemed to Katy to last for hours, and she wanted it to never end. But eventually they came up for air, and Katy knelt on the floor of the stall and took Sir Charles's long weapon in her hand and kissed the knob of it, opening her mouth wide to take it in, and tongue the tiny hole in the end. Sir Charles stood, feet astride, above her, leant back against the side of the shower, closed his eyes with his head up, letting the water beat down on his face as she sucked him off.

Katy delicately took his balls between her fingers and squeezed them until he moaned with pleasure. She sucked and tongued him harder, and after a few minutes she felt his balls jump in her hands and he shot his load into her mouth. It felt as if he had half a pint of jism between his legs, and she swallowed every drop, savouring the sweet, salty taste of the thick cream that filled her mouth.

24

When Katy had swallowed the last delicious drop of male essence from Sir Charles's prick, he reached up and turned off the cascade of water from the shower spigot.

'Good,' he said. 'Very good. Now dry me.'

Katy got up from her knees and fetched one of the giant, fluffy, white bath sheets from where it had been warming on a rail and dried her new lover and herself, peeling off her sopping wet panties as she went, and throwing them onto the floor.

When she and Sir Charles were dry, she used one of the combs that lay on the shelf above the washbasin to pull her still damp hair back from her forehead, and he led her out of the bathroom, both of them still naked, and over to the long leather sofa where he pulled her down onto his lap and they kissed again. Their kisses were deep and passionate, and Katy could feel the juice oozing out from her cunt, and Sir Charles's prick became hard again, jutting up between her naked thighs as she moved round on him to allow it the freedom it needed to grow, until he laid her flat on her back and mounted her. The knob of his cock felt enormous as it pushed at the opening of her love canal, and she reached down and positioned his helmet perfectly for his first thrust into her tender hole. As he entered, she almost screamed with pleasure. This was the knob she wanted. The one that could complete the circle between her legs and make her whole. A real woman at last, with her man inside her.

She relaxed her cunt muscles as his enormous member pushed deeper, until she thought she'd burst from the sheer size of it; if she didn't burst with pleasure first. When his penis was fully embedded in her body, Sir Charles shifted his weight to his elbows and moved his forearms under her shoulders and started to move inside her. He pulled his cock almost all the way out of her cunt, then pushed it back in hard. Katy was in paradise. A paradise she never wanted to leave, as he continued to pull out and push into her. She linked her ankles across his back, and their mouths met again, their tongues entwining as he began to move faster, and her whole body suffused with the pleasure of their love making.

Faster he went, and faster still, until the sweat broke out on both their bodies, and Katy felt her back sticking to the leather upholstery where they lay, and still they didn't stop. They matched each other stroke for stroke as their screwing became more frenzied, and Katy could hardly breathe with his mouth glued to hers.

Finally, as Sir Charles's strokes became shorter, and he pulled her harder to him, she felt the heat of her climax start deep down inside her womb and begin to fill her body, until she had to pull her mouth away from his and scream in ecstasy as her orgasm finally burst through every pleasure centre of her brain. She called out for him to shoot her with his come, which was her middle-aged lover's signal to empty the heavy sacs between his legs into her womb for the first time.

25

Katy and Sir Charles lay together on the sofa as the sweat dried on their bodies.

'That was wonderful,' she said.

Sir Charles looked into her face. 'I've rogered many a wench on this sofa, but you were far and away the best, Miss Dunn,' he said.

'Rogered the wench,' said Katy. 'Is that what you just did?'

'Yes.'

'I like that,' she said. 'Yes, I think I like being rogered by you.'

'But I think now we'd better get dressed,' said Sir Charles. 'We have work to do.' He kissed her briefly, and they both got up. Sir Charles walked naked to a cupboard at the back of the office that Katy knew from her investigations on Monday morning was kept locked. On the way he collected his key ring from the desk and used one of the small keys on it to open the cupboard. Inside hung a number of fresh white shirts, two dark suits and a number of ties. On the shelves at the side were socks, handkerchiefs and underwear. On the floor, neatly lined up, were several pairs of black shoes.

'Would you bring my other clothes in with you when you're dressed,' asked Sir Charles.

Katy went back into the bathroom. She found the hair drier and blew her hair almost dry, then got dressed again. Her knickers were still soaking so she left them off, and carried them and Sir Charles's clothes back into his office. By that time Sir Charles was as immaculate as ever in his office attire and waiting for her.

'I'll have to go without panties today,' she said as she gave him his stuff and he tossed it into the cupboard and re-locked the door. 'Mine are still wet from the shower and I don't have a spare pair with me.'

'Very nice too, Miss Dunn,' he said. 'I'll have to investigate that when you're taking dictation. Which will be in . . .' He looked at his watch. 'Half an hour exactly. I have some calls to make.'

'Will you roger me again soon?' asked Katy shamelessly.

Sir Charles smiled and kissed her on the cheek. 'Of course I will, Miss Dunn,' he replied. 'We haven't even started yet.'

Katy went into her office, sat down, balled up her wet knickers and put them into her desk drawer, right at the back. I'll keep those just as they are as a souvenir, she thought. I've plenty more at home.

Half an hour later she returned to Sir Charles's office where he was just putting down his phone. 'Perfect timing,' he said. 'I've just finished.'

'I like it when our timing's right,' said Katy cheekily, and picked up her pad and pencil from where she'd left them on the corner of his desk earlier, and went and sat down on Sir Charles's lap.

143

'What do you want me to take down?' she asked.

Sir Charles laughed out loud. 'You're a shameless hussy,' he said. 'And I don't think you're wearing what I want you to take down any more. I think you've taken them down already.' And he kissed her full on the mouth. The kiss lengthened as his hand crept up between her thighs, over the tops of her stockings, up the thin straps of her suspenders and to the dampness of her naked cunt, which opened like a flower to his questing fingers. Katy shifted to allow her skirt to ride up her thighs and her legs to open wider. She sank back against his chest as he found her clitoris and began to rub it gently. Katy moaned as he teased the stiff little organ of pleasure from the folds of skin that protected it from harm, and she felt her hot blood engorge it like a tiny penis.

'Oh, Sir Charles,' she whispered. 'That feels so good. Please don't stop.'

'Shall I give you dictation, or shall I give you something else?' he asked.

'Give me something else.'

'What, exactly?' he teased.

'You know.'

'No, I don't.'

'Do you want me to beg for it?'

'Yes.' Just like Daphne had said, she thought.

'Give me a fuck,' she pleaded. 'I'm dying for it.'

Sir Charles smiled down at her, pulled his hand out from under her skirt and eased her off his knee. 'On the desk,' he said. 'Pull your skirt up and sit on the edge.'

She did as he said, and hoisted her skirt up around her waist to show off her stockings, suspenders and her naked pussy, which glistened with pearly drops of lubrication in its matted hair.

Sir Charles knelt between her open thighs and tongued at her sopping wet cunt, much as Katy had knelt before him in the shower stall. His tongue felt gigantic to her as it invaded her private parts, and he nibbled at the lips of the hairy, open mouth between her legs. Time stood still for them both as he gammed her. And when his face was covered in their love juice from their first fuck, and the honey that she was producing for another, he stood, lowered the zipper of his trousers and allowed his cock freedom. He pushed her back onto the desk and stood between her legs, bending his knees until his knob end was rubbing her pubic hair. He positioned his rod and pushed it into her greasy love tunnel and took her hands and pulled her towards him over the top of the desk so that her cunt slid up the length of his cock. Katy gasped as he did it. She'd never known such fun and bent her legs and put her heels behind his thighs as they coupled. Sir Charles put the palms of his hands flat on the desk and slid in and out of her as she lay looking up at the ceiling, tightening and loosening the muscles of her cervix as he screwed her.

'I'm going to come,' he panted, flicking his hair off his forehead.

'Wait for me,' she pleaded.

'I can't.'

'You can.' And Katy gritted her teeth as she felt her second orgasm of the day rip through her body and he stood stock still and again released his jism into her womb.

26

Katy lay back on the desk as Sir Charles withdrew his cock from her cunt. As he did so, she could feel their juices running out of her open vagina onto the polished wood where she lay.

'You're quite a girl, Miss Dunn,' he said. 'I thought as much the first time I saw you.'

Katy leaned up on one elbow. 'I thought you hadn't noticed me.'

'Not at all. My John Thomas got quite hard. I wanted you there and then, and promised myself that I would have you.'

Katy stood up, pulled down her skirt and smoothed the material down over her legs, feeling another thrill as the come in her cunt dribbled down her naked thighs. 'And now you have. Twice.'

'And will again.'

'Of course,' she said. 'Any time you want me. I'm your secretary after all. Your property to do with as you please.'

'That's the ticket,' said Sir Charles. 'A girl after my own heart.'

And your heart is what I shall have, vowed Katy.

'Are we going to do the dictation?' she asked.

'That can wait,' he said. 'I think lunch would be much more in order.'

'But I'm a mess,' protested Katy. 'If this happens again I'll have to have some fresh clothes to change into myself.'

'You look gorgeous,' said Sir Charles. 'Ravishing. Or ravished at least.' And he laughed out loud again. 'I'll book a table at my favourite place, and we'll take a long lunch. Bring your stuff and you can go straight home afterwards. I'll get Hartley to drop you off.'

'Very well, Sir Charles,' said Katy, and within five minutes they were on their way.

They lunched at a secluded table in a very fancy restaurant just off Bond Street, where Sir Charles was obviously well known, and Katy was treated like a queen. He insisted that she sat next to him, and before long he asked Katy to pull up her skirt so that he could finger her pussy between courses. Each time he did, he licked his fingers and declared the taste better than the food. Katy was horny again before the entrée arrived, and Sir Charles promised her a treat on the way home.

Whilst he was signing for the bill, Sir Charles got the maitre d' to call Hartley on the phone in the car, and the chauffeur was waiting outside by the kerb with the rear door open when they emerged from the restaurant.

'Drive us through Hyde Park,' ordered Sir Charles when Harvey was back behind the wheel. Which he did, and when the car crunched across Rotten Row, Sir Charles said, 'Can you find somewhere to park?' Hartley stopped at a meter on South Carriage Drive. 'Half an hour,' said Sir Charles when the car was stationary, and Hartley got out, put some money in the meter, and walked into the park proper.

Sir Charles turned to Katy, gathered her up in his arms and kissed her. 'I can't resist you, you little slut,' he said as he ran one hand through the luxuriant fall of blonde hair at the back of her neck.

'Sir Charles,' said Katy, 'someone will see.

'No, they won't. And even if they do, who cares? I promised you a treat and I intend to give you one.'

Not literally, thought Katy as she responded to his caresses. What will people think?

Sir Charles cupped her breasts through her blouse and bra. He could remember the feeling as he had caressed those darling young globes when they had showered together, and he longed to suck the pert pinkness of her nipples until they turned bright red as they filled with blood, and felt his prick rise at the thought. Four times in one day, he mused. Not bad for a man my age.

Katy felt it rise too, as she ran her fingers over the wool worsted of his suit trousers. My God, but you're insatiable, *she* thought. Not bad for a man your age.

Then he ran his hand down her body and along her thighs until he reached the hem of her short skirt.

Uppsa-daisy, thought Katy as his hand went under the material and made its cheeky journey up between her legs to the delights of her cunt, which Katy thought must be deliciously smelly by now, with all the sex it had had that day.

'Sir Charles,' she said into the material of his jacket as she put her head on his chest. 'You are naughty.'

'I want to make you come again before I take you home so that you'll think of me tonight,' he whispered.

'I would anyway,' said Katy. 'You must know that.'

'I just want to be sure,' he said, as he tickled her clitoris and rubbed the damp lips of her pussy between his fingers.

Pleasure ran through Katy's body like a thousand tiny electric shocks, as Sir Charles's fingers continued to probe and stroke her private parts. Her skirt was up high enough for both of them to watch him pet her pussy, and by then Katy didn't care if anyone did see what they were doing through the tinted windows of the limousine. In fact it would have made it more exciting if people had been watching.

She writhed all over the back seat of the car under Sir Charles's ministrations, calling out for him to frig her harder between planting kisses all over his face, and glueing her mouth to his. Suddenly she felt the pleasure concentrate inside her womb and she knew that her orgasm was close, and she clamped her thighs tightly on his hand and rode his fingers to the most satisfying come of the day so far.

27

When Hartley returned from his walk, shortly after, and resumed his seat behind the wheel without as much as a glance into the back of the car, the soul of discretion that he was, Sir Charles told him to head for Waterloo, where Katy was dropped off at the top of her road with just a brief, chaste kiss from her new lover.

When she got into the flat she sat on the sofa and put her feet up. Suddenly she felt wiped out. It had been one of those days, and as she relaxed she replayed her sexual adventures through her mind and immediately started feeling horny again.

About half an hour later, still lying with her head comfortably on a cushion, her skirt up, and her fingers absent-mindedly playing with her clitoris, remembering the way Sir Charles's cock had pumped into her pussy, she heard Mark's key in the door.

Christ! she thought, I should have had a shower and changed. I bet he'll smell the sex on me, and she jumped up to greet him.

'Hello, darling,' said Mark, as he entered the room, dropped his briefcase on the floor and tossed his raincoat across the back of a chair. 'Come and give me a kiss.'

Katy did as he asked, feeling just slightly guilty at what had occurred with Sir Charles, and the fact that she was two-timing Mark. She knew that getting involved with her boss was wrong, and that he was probably just using her, but her attraction for the older man and the excitement it engendered made her ignore any twinge of conscience that she felt.

Mark kissed her hard and pushed her back towards the sofa.

Oh Christ, she thought, he wants a fuck. And so, she realised did she. I'm getting so naughty she thought, as Mark bore her down onto the seat and started to undo the buttons of her blouse.

He freed her breasts from the constraint of her bra cups, and began to suck at her nipples sending a glorious warm glow down to her naked pussy.

Oh my God, I've got no knickers on, realised Katy. He's bound to notice *that*.

And indeed he did as he slid his hands up her thighs where Sir Charles's had wandered such a short time before, revealing the tops of her stockings stained with the juice that had leaked out of Katy's slit.

'No panties,' he said. 'What's all this?'

'I wanted to wee on the way home,' improvised Katy. 'I couldn't wait and I dribbled. My knickers were so wet I chucked them into the washing.'

'You're very wet now, I must say,' said Mark, finding the entrance to her cunt. 'I wonder what it tastes like.' He slid off the sofa, pushed her skirt up further, knelt down between her legs and pushed his face into her bush.

It felt quite delightful to Katy as his tongue explored her. He's drinking Sir Charles's and my come, she thought excitedly. I hope he doesn't see the spunk on my stocking tops.

But Mark was too excited by the delicious musky taste of Katy's pussy to notice anything else. He'd never tasted anything so delicious as the juice that flowed freely from her tunnel of love, and he lapped it up like a baby at its mother's breast.

He stood up and undressed quickly. As Katy lay looking up at him, she unfastened her skirt, pushed it down her legs and unbuttoned her blouse to allow him free access to her firm young body.

I'm going to have two men's come inside me at the same time she thought, as she opened her legs wide to allow Mark to lay between them. This is the best day of my life.

When he was fitted comfortably in the cleft that she made with her thighs, Katy's questing fingers found the solid meat of his prick and she squirmed around until it fitted into the hole between her legs. They coupled. She moaned as his hugeness filled the aching void that was her pussy. Part of the ache was her need, and part the soreness from her sexual exertions with Sir Charles earlier.

Mark pushed himself deeper inside her, and she responded by pushing her hips up to meet his in the ancient movements of love that she was beginning to learn so well.

They rocked together on the sofa, Katy's cunt muscles stroking Mark's cock as it slid in and out of her, and the tightly stretched skin that sheathed it felt like hot silk inside Katy's velvet hole.

'Shoot me,' she cried, as their screw got wilder, and Mark's lips stretched back over his teeth as he concentrated on pounding her harder and harder into the cushions. 'Shoot me darling. I'm dry and need your spunk.'

'You're not dry,' he whispered. 'You're soaking.'

'Not wet enough. Not nearly enough. I need you to make me wetter.'

Her words drove Mark to fresh paroxysms of passion, and he thudded his body against hers until she felt as if his cock would ream the soft membranes in her cunt. But still she cried for him to fuck her harder.

'Roger me,' she screamed almost out of her mind with passion. Remembering Sir Charles's words and how they'd affected her. 'Roger me, you bastard.'

At those words, Mark pushed himself as deeply inside her as he ever had, and froze as the jism jetted out of his prick and splashed up inside Katy so hard that it was as if a hose-pipe full of hot water had been forced up inside her.

'Good,' she screamed. 'That's so good.' And she came herself, and drenched his penis with her own warm juice.

28

When Katy got into the office the next day she found a message waiting on her desk. Sir Charles had been called away suddenly on business and would not be back until Monday morning.

Damn it, she thought. And I wore my new lemon-coloured undies specially.

For the remainder of Thursday and all day Friday Katy sat in her office and finished the book she'd found in her desk, and started another that she purchased at Thursday lunchtime. The phone rarely rang and there was no work for her to do. Although she was bored, she was being paid for her time, and at least she had her Friday night out with Daphne to look forward to.

At six p.m. precisely that evening, Katy met her friend in the foyer of the building, and they made the short journey to the wine bar they had chosen, on foot.

Even though it was relatively early when they arrived, the place was already crowded, and all the male heads in the place followed their progress as they headed for the bar. 'Some decent talent in already tonight,' said Daphne as they slid onto two empty stools. 'And it doesn't start to buzz in here for an hour or so, from what've I've heard. What do you want to drink?'

'It's my shout,' said Katy. 'Two bottles of champagne, I think.'

'I won't hold you to the bet,' said Daphne. 'If you don't think you lost.'

'I didn't the other day, but I do now.' And Katy blushed slightly under her friend's gaze.

Daphne's jaw dropped as she realised what Katy was saying. '*Katy!*' she exclaimed. 'He didn't? . . . he did. I told you he would.'

'He certainly did,' said Katy, blushing even deeper. 'You were right.'

'What happened?' demanded Daphne. 'You promised you'd tell.'

'That's why we're here. I've got to tell someone. But you must promise to keep it a secret.'

'Cross my heart,' said Daphne.

At that point the barman approached them. 'A bottle of champagne and two glasses,' said Katy, and laid a twenty-pound note on the counter.

'Celebrating girls?' asked the barman with a cheeky grin as he got the freezing bottle from the huge bucket of ice where it had sat with its companions.

'You could say that,' said Katy. 'My friend won a bet.'

'But I think *my* friend got the best of the deal,' added Daphne.

'Congratulations,' said the barman as he removed the cork with nothing more than a gentle pop, filled two chilled champagne flutes, and put the cash in the till.

'Come on,' said Daphne, picking up her glass and the bottle. 'Let's sit down at that table in the corner. I want to be comfortable when you tell me the whole story.'

Katy picked up her own glass and followed her friend to the secluded table she had referred to, next to one of the walls of the wine bar, and partially shaded by a huge cheese plant.

When they were sitting comfortably, Daphne and Katy raised their glasses and clinked them together. 'To sin,' said Daphne.

'Sin,' echoed Katy, and pulled a self-conscious face.

When they had sipped their drinks and Daphne had lit a cigarette, she said. 'Come on then Katy. Spill the beans.'

Katy told her everything. From Sir Charles's orders that Katy should wash him in the shower, the blow job that she'd given him after she'd done it, their fuck on the desk, and Katy's orgasm in the back of the Jaguar, followed by her delicious screw with cousin Mark when she'd ended up with two men's jism in her pussy.

'Do you think I'm awful?' she asked, when she had finished her tale.

'I think you're a lucky bitch,' said Daphne. 'I'm getting horny at the very thought of it. Ordering you into the shower. I just *love* being ordered about by men. Then over the desk, and in the back of his car. I've seen that car. I wish he'd get me in the back of it, I'd have him naked in a minute.'

'I'm sure he wouldn't object,' said Katy. 'But I'm sure your husband would.'

'And your boyfriend wouldn't if he knew?'

'We're not married,' said Katy. Although truth to tell she did feel a bit bad about the way she was deceiving Mark.

'Why did you have to remind me that I am?' pouted Daphne. 'Especially when those two hunky blokes over there have been staring at us since we sat down.'

'Which two?' asked Katy, looking round.

'Don't look,' hissed Daphne. 'We don't want them to think we're interested. It's the two by the bar, right at the end. One's wearing a flashy blue suit, the other's in a tan mac.'

Katy gave it a few seconds then glanced round and saw the two men Daphne was talking about. They were both about twenty-five, smartly dressed and good-looking.

'They're nice,' she said. 'Are they really looking over here?'

'They are.'

'What shall we do?'

'See what happens.'

And what happened was that the barman appeared with another bottle of champagne. 'Compliments of the two gentlemen in the corner,' he said with a cheeky grin. 'It looks like it's your lucky night, girls.'

'Will you ask them to join us?' said Daphne, and Katy felt her jaw drop.

'Daphne,' she said, after the barman had vanished on his task. 'What are you doing?'

'They're tasty,' said Daphne. 'They've obviously got a few bob. They want to buy us a drink. Why not ask them over? Where's the harm? If we don't fancy them, we do a runner.'

'OK,' said Katy after a moment's thought. 'But don't leave me alone with either of them.'

'OK,' said Daphne. 'I promise. Look out, here they come. Smile, honey, you're on candid camera.'

The two young men walked up to Katy and Daphne's table and both grinned down at the young women. 'Hello,' said the one in the blue suit. 'My name's Kenny, this is Dave.'

29

'Hi,' said Daphne. 'I'm Daphne, and this is my friend Katy. Thanks for the champagne.'

'Daphne, Katy,' said Kenny. 'We hate to see two lovely young women buying their own drinks. We'd much rather treat them.'

'That's very kind of you. We appreciate it,' said Daphne. 'Won't you sit down?'

'Don't mind if we do,' said Kenny. He pulled up two chairs from an adjoining table, and he and Dave sat down.

'Do you work round here?' asked Dave.

'Up the road,' replied Daphne. 'At International House.'

'Big time,' said Dave. 'The oil business.'

'Not really,' replied Daphne. 'I'm just in the typing pool, though Katy here is a director's secretary.'

'Blimey,' said Kenny. 'You don't look old enough.'

'She's got talent,' said Daphne, and Katy blushed at the remark, and the double meaning that Daphne gave it. 'What do you two do?'

'Money brokers,' said Dave. 'The last of the yuppies.'

'Not the "Y" word,' said Kenny. 'It'll get you

banned out of a place like this if anyone hears it these days.' And both the young men laughed.

'Porsches and Armani?' said Daphne.

'Not any more. More like an Escort van and Marks and Sparks, but we survive,' said Kenny.

'Laughing our way through the recession,' said Dave, and poured himself more champagne. 'Here's to it. Life after the crash.' And all four touched glasses.

'So what are you two doing tonight?' asked Kenny.

'Nothing much,' replied Daphne. 'Just having a quiet drink at the end of a hard working week.'

'Want to do something?' asked Dave.

Daphne shrugged. 'Could do. Like what?'

'Like get pissed on champagne,' said Kenny. 'And have some fun.'

'What kind of fun?' asked Daphne.

'Who knows?' said Kenny with a wink. 'Let's get pissed and find out.'

'I'm a married woman,' said Daphne.

'Is your husband here?' asked Dave, looking round in an exaggerated way.

Daphne smiled. 'No. Not tonight.'

'Well, if you don't tell him, we won't.' said Dave. 'And how about your friend here? Doesn't she speak? Is she married, or what?'

'Leave her alone, Dave,' interrupted Kenny. 'She's like the Mona Lisa. Still waters and all that. Enigmatic. She'll speak when she's good and ready, won't you, Katy? And she's not wearing a wedding ring *or* an engagement ring. Looks like she's young, free and single. Just like us.' And he gave her the benefit of a charming smile that Katy found both infectious and exciting.

'That's right,' she said. 'I'll speak when I'm ready. And Kenny's correct. I *am* young free and single, and I *do* fancy drinking champagne with you two and having some fun tonight.'

'See, Dave,' said Kenny. 'Told you didn't I? These two are girls after our own hearts.' He picked up his glass and toasted the table. 'And here's to us.'

'To us,' the other three echoed.

By ten-thirty, the four of them had consumed six bottles of champagne between them and the party was hotting up.

'How about going round to my place?' said Kenny. 'It's more comfortable than here, and there's plenty of booze. We can get a cab and be there in less than fifteen minutes.'

'Where is it? asked Daphne.

'Clapham Common. North side.'

'Not a bad idea,' she said. 'I live just off the Wandsworth Road. It's close enough to walk home.'

'If you want to go home,' said Dave.

'We will,' said Daphne firmly. 'What do you say Katy?'

'I'm game,' replied Katy. 'But I can't stay too late.'

'Nor me,' said Daphne. 'But a quick drink can't do any harm.'

'And I'll spring for the cab,' said Dave. 'So you get a free ride home. How about you Katy, where do you live?'

'Waterloo.'

'Katy can come back to my place and get a cab from there,' said Daphne.

'Fine,' said Kenny. 'Let's finish this bottle and go.'

Which they did, and caught a cruising taxi within a

minute or two, and were outside the house where Kenny's flat was situated ten minutes later.

Kenny let them in and up the stairs to his door. Inside was a comfortable if untidy bachelor pad which he explained had a lounge, two bedrooms, kitchen and bathroom.

'Do you want to help me sort out the glasses?' he said to Katy when he'd taken everyone's coats and hung them on a rack just inside the front door.

Katy nodded, and he said, 'Kitchen's this way. Dave, Daphne, go into the lounge and put on some music. Dave knows where everything is.'

Dave opened one of the doors off the hall and switched on the light, then stepped back to allow Daphne to enter, and Kenny took Katy's hand and led her down to the kitchen where he got two bottles out of the fridge and opened them. 'Glasses are in the cupboard there,' he said, and Katy opened it and found four clean glasses.

'Do you live here on your own?' she asked.

'Yes. Dave stays sometimes if he's up in town late. He lives in Crawley of all God-forsaken places. He'll stay tonight. Otherwise I'm here alone.'

'No girlfriend?' asked Katy.

Kenny shook his head. 'No one special. Occasionally I get lucky, you know how it is . . .'

Katy knew exactly how it was.

'Do you think you've got lucky tonight?'

He shrugged. 'Who knows?'

Who knows indeed? thought Katy, but she had an idea from the warmth she was feeling between her legs that he might have.

They took the bottles and glasses back into the

dimly lit living room, where they found Dave and Daphne on the sofa together, snogging heavily to the sound of Aretha Franklin on the stereo.

'Don't let us interrupt anything,' said Kenny as they entered.

Daphne looked up and said. 'You won't.'

'Drink anyone?' asked Kenny.

Everyone concurred, and Kenny filled four glasses and passed them round.

Katy sat down in the armchair that matched the sofa and Kenny perched on the arm.

'Wanna dance?' asked Dave, and he dragged Daphne to her feet and they began to move slowly, wrapped together, to the music.

'How about you Katy?' said Kenny.

'Sure,' said Katy, placing her glass on the floor next to the chair and standing up.

Kenny put his glass next to hers, stood up too, and took her in his arms. The music was slow and gentle and Katy moved in close to Kenny's body, and felt his erection press into her tummy. It felt good and she moved herself slowly against it, feeling it lengthen and thicken against the softness of her body.

Kenny kissed her then for the first time. A long, slow, deep kiss that went with the wine they'd consumed, and the music and the soft lighting in the room. Katy returned the kiss, feeling dizzy and leaning against Kenny as she did it.

'OK?' he whispered, when they broke the kiss.

'Wonderful,' said Katy.

'Come into my room. It's more comfortable there.'

'Alright.'

He took her hand and led her out of the lounge.

Daphne and Dave were barely moving to the music by then, and kissing so deeply themselves that they didn't notice Katy and Kenny leave. They went down the hall to another door which Kenny opened, and in the light from the hall Katy saw the corner of a double bed. He walked around the side of it and switched on a bedside lamp. In its soft glow she saw Kenny pull back the duvet. He walked over and shut the door, and they stood looking at each other.

'Come here,' he said, and Katy went into his arms again, and they kissed for the second time.

Kenny's erection was even fuller by then, but trapped inside his trousers which, although they were on the baggy side, did prevent it from rearing up away from his body as Katy knew it wanted to do. She felt his hands move down to her buttocks and find the crack between and she moaned softly and writhed against him harder.

He pulled up her skirt. Sliding it up her thighs until his fingers found the naked flesh between her panties and her stocking tops. What colour knickers am I wearing? she thought. Oh yes, the strawberry-coloured ones. I wonder what he'll make of those?

'Stockings,' he said. 'I thought as much.'

'You dirty boy,' said Katy. 'Were you peeping?'

'I was trying to,' admitted Kenny. 'But you kept your knees together.'

'Just as well,' said Katy. 'But now you know.'

'I do, don't I?' said Kenny. 'I love stockings, they're so much sexier than ugly old tights.'

'I know they are,' replied Katy. 'That's why I wear them. All men seem to love stockings.'

'Who can blame them?' said Kenny. 'Especially

when someone with legs like yours wears them,' and he moved his hands up to the elastic top of her knickers and slid his fingers underneath it and onto her bare buttocks. 'You've got a great arse too,' he commented.

'Thank you, kind sir. Yours is not too bad either.'

Kenny gently pushed Katy towards the bed and she stepped out of her shoes as she went. He laid her down, took off his jacket and joined her. She pulled her jacket off and threw it across a chair at the far side of the bed, and Kenny tugged off his tie, then started to unbutton Katy's blouse to reveal her creamy breasts which were bursting out of the strawberry-coloured lace bra that confined them.

'I like your undies,' he said. 'Are they silk?'

She nodded, and he undid the rest of her buttons, pulled the tails of her blouse out of her skirt and pushed the garment off her shoulders. They kissed again then, and Kenny's hands cupped her tits through the lace of her brassiere until he reached round and undid the clip at the back, to free the milk-white orbs tipped with rose pink to his greedy gaze.

'You're beautiful,' he said, and put his head down and fastened his lips on the right nipple and gently sucked it to rigidity.

Katy felt a thrill in her womb as his tongue licked around the aureole of her nipple, and she put her hand down into his lap and found the long, hard length of his prick.

Kenny moaned as her hand found his tool, and she reached for the tab of the zipper at his fly, and eased it down slowly, then reached inside. Underneath his suit trousers he was wearing boxer shorts and she put her fingers in through the gap at the front and allowed his cock to pop out and into her waiting palm. His knob was long, hard and hot, and she gently rolled the foreskin right back and put her head down to the helmet.

Kenny moaned again, louder this time as she wet his prick with her saliva and took the first two inches inside her mouth and sucked hard.

'God,' he said. 'You're great.'

She sucked him for a minute or two as he rubbed her breasts, then pulled away and undid the top button of his trousers.

'Get undressed,' she said. 'I want to see you naked.'

'You too,' said Kenny, and without any more ado Katy undid the button on her skirt and unzipped the fastener. She pulled the skirt over her hips and undid her stockings from their suspenders, unhitched the belt and finally slid her briefs off and tossed them on top of her other clothes, as Kenny stood up and undressed himself, watching her every move as he did it.

When she was naked, he turned away to pull off his boxers and throw them on the floor, and she looked at the smooth, tanned skin of his body in the dim, apricot-coloured light from the bedside lamp.

She could see the sharply defined muscles on his back and arms, his high, tight buttocks and his long, strong legs and she felt herself melt inside at the thought of being loved by him. Then he turned, and for the first time she saw properly his genitals. His cock was long and swollen, jutting out from the dark bush of his pubic hair which almost, but but not quite, hid the fullness of the sacs that hung between his legs. She gasped at the beauty of his sex, and felt the juices flowing from hers to lubricate the entry of his cock.

He joined her on the bed and they embraced and as he cupped her breasts she felt his knob bang against her thigh and saw a drop of semen emerge from the tiny hole at the end, stick to her skin and stretch like elastic as he moved away. She put her fingers down, caught the juice from his prick and licked it from her fingers.

They kissed, and their tongues explored each other's mouths, and their teeth bit at each other's lips before Kenny slid down the length of her body and attached his mouth to that other pair of wet lips, those between her legs.

His tongue flicked in and out of her love canal, and he found her clitoris with his teeth and nibbled at the enlarged piece of gristle until she cried out for him to stop, it felt so good.

But he didn't. Egged on by her cries he opened his mouth and took her entire mound of venus into his mouth and sucked the juices back into his throat.

Still with her cunt in his mouth, Katy slid round until her face was level with his prick and she took it into *her* mouth and swallowed it down until his glans were rubbing the back of her throat, and she felt that she might choke at any minute. But instead of letting it out, she tried to swallow it deeper.

They sixty-nined for what seemed like an eternity to Katy, sucking and licking until all that Katy could hear was the sounds of enjoyment they both made as they feasted on each other's sex.

Kenny was the first to break away, and he plucked Katy from her position and their saliva-filled mouths joined in a long, wet kiss, which once again seemed to last forever. Then Kenny rolled over until he was on top of her, and she guided his prick into her wide-open cunt and they were one.

Their fuck started slow and controlled, but neither could curb their urgency, and soon they were thrashing at each other's bodies as if demented. Kenny held her hands beside her head, and beat at her with his hips, and she returned the movements until she felt there was a danger his cock would spring out of her over-lubricated cunt, or the bed would break beneath them.

But neither of her fears were realised, and as the sweat poured off their bodies she heard him calling out her name and she knew that he was close to climax.

'Wait,' she screamed, 'wait.' And he paused, just long enough for her to feel the orgasm burst through her body before he pumped his spunk into her hole.

30

Kenny and Katy lay together on the bed for a few minutes, Kenny's hand gently caressing Katy's thigh. 'We'd better go and find Daphne,' she said eventually.

'You're not going to go, are you?' said Kenny.

'We'll have to.'

'Please stay.'

'No. I can't.'

'Can I see you again?'

'Maybe.'

'Give me your phone number.'

'No. Give me yours.'

Kenny hunted round for paper and a pencil whilst Katy hurriedly got dressed. She mopped up as much spunk from her pussy as she could, but still felt it dribbling into her panties when she put them on.

Kenny gave her a sheet of paper with his work and home numbers on it and Katy stuffed it into the pocket of her jacket as he also got dressed.

Shame, she thought as he covered his beautiful body with his clothing. But I've got bigger fish to fry.

When they were both fully dressed they went back down the hall to the living room where they found Dave and Daphne in congress on the sofa.

Dave was thrusting his body into Daphne's and Katy stood transfixed in the doorway at the sight, feeling her pussy juices starting to flow again as she watched her friend and a stranger fucking each other. She could see Daphne's dark-skinned body responding to Dave's, and she noticed that the nipples on her tiny breasts, which kept popping in and out of sight, were the same size and colour as chocolate buttons.

Daphne looked up over Dave's shoulder and winked. Katy grabbed Kenny and dragged him along to the kitchen.

'I wanted to watch,' he said.

'How would you like it?' she asked.

He shrugged. 'I wouldn't mind,' he said, and Katy's juices started flowing even faster.

'You're a dirty pig,' she said.

'So I am,' and he grabbed her and pulled her down onto his lap on one of the kitchen chairs. They snogged happily until Daphne came into the room, fully dressed herself.

'We'd better go,' she said.

'Do you have to?' asked Kenny, dragging his mouth away from Katy's.

'I do. I'm a married woman. I already told you that.'

'You wouldn't know it from the way you were carrying on in there.'

Daphne smiled. 'That's my business. Are you coming Katy? Or staying here?'

Katy was tempted to stay with Kenny, but was a good enough friend not to leave Daphne to get home alone, and reluctantly got off Kenny's lap. 'I'm coming,' she said.

They all three went back into the living room where Dave was lying on the sofa, dressed only in his underpants, through which Katy could clearly see the outline of his cock. 'You both off?' he said. 'Shame. I'll see you next week, right, Daphne?'

'We'll see,' said Daphne, who leant down and kissed him briefly. 'Come on, Katy. Let's go.'

Katy kissed Kenny goodbye, and he begged her to call him, before she followed her friend out of the flat, down the stairs and into the street.

'This way,' said Daphne, pointing towards the centre of London. 'It's only a few minutes' walk to my place.'

'Are you going to see Dave again?' asked Katy, as they walked in the direction that Daphne had indicated, their heels echoing on the empty pavements.

'Dunno. Maybe. He said he'd be in that wine bar next Friday night. I might go, I might not. I don't know if I fancy it. He's got a nice cock, but ...' She didn't finish the sentence, then asked. 'What about you?'

'I've got Kenny's number. He hasn't got mine.'

'Wise girl,' said Daphne, and they turned off the main road by the common onto a side street which led in the direction of Lavender Hill.

Within a few minutes Daphne had dug a set of keys out of her handbag, 'That's the one over there, on the corner.' They crossed over to a four-storied, end-of-terrace house within sight of the Wandsworth Road.

'Come on through,' said Daphne, when she'd opened the door and put on the light in the hall.

'Won't we disturb your husband?' the younger girl asked as she crossed the threshold, and they walked down the hall to the living room where Daphne switched on a couple of table lamps to softly illuminate the room.

'Don't you remember? I told you he's away until

the morning on business. Him and that damn business of his. It's no wonder I look elsewhere for a bit of fun.'

'We were naughty, weren't we?' said Katy, sitting down on the sofa.

'Yes,' agreed Daphne. 'Especially you. What a week you've had. First Sir Charles, then Kenny, and you've still got your cousin at home ready to give you a service when you need it. Whatever next?'

'I don't know.' said Katy.

'Do you want some coffee before I call you a cab?' asked Daphne.

'Sure,' said Katy, and Daphne went through to the kitchen to put on the kettle.

'Do you want a brandy with it?' she called.

'Haven't we drunk enough?'

'The night's still young,' said Daphne, coming through with a bottle and two glasses. 'You're not in any rush are you?'

'No. I said I'd be late. I told Mark I was going out with a girlfriend from work.'

'And a couple of boyfriends, as it turned out,' said Daphne, as she poured two large measures of spirit and gave one to Katy. 'Want to see the rest of the place? We've got two floors of this desirable converted residence.'

'Sure,' said Katy, who got up from the sofa and followed her hostess out into the hall, both holding their glasses.

'There's the dining room here,' said Daphne, opening the door opposite. 'And the kitchen's at the very end. Very modern. Then the bedrooms, bathroom and toilet are upstairs. Come on, I'll show you.'

Katy followed Daphne's neat behind in its tight skirt

as they climbed the flights of stairs.

'This is the bathroom and loo, in case you need it.' Daphne opened the first door on the right. 'The spare room's the one on the left. And our room is down at the end. Come on in,' she invited, as she led the way.

Katy followed Daphne into the master bedroom of the flat, and Daphne touched a switch by the door that sparked the dim bulbs of two lamps behind their dusty pink shades, one each side of a large double bed.

Daphne sat down on the edge of the mattress and said, 'I must take off my knickers. They're soaking. How about yours?'

Katy nodded in an embarrassed way. 'Don't be shy,' said Daphne. 'We both know what we've been up to with those guys. I saw the pair of you peeping. Was yours good?'

Katy smiled and nodded again.

'So was mine,' said Daphne. 'He had a lovely big one. Maybe I will meet him next week after all. I'm getting randy again just thinking about him. Did yours have one as nice as Sir Charles's?'

'It was different,' replied Katy, and watched as Daphne hitched up her skirt above the tops of her dark nylons and pulled down the brief black panties she was wearing, revealing a tight bush of oily black hair between her legs. The older woman examined the inside of them and licked the contents. 'Mmm ... Nice,' she said. 'Come and see.'

Katy did as she was told, and saw that the gusset of Daphne's knickers was thick with transparent goo.

'I love come,' said Daphne. 'Let me see yours.'

Katy hesitated, wide-eyed at Daphne's request.

'Come on,' said Daphne. 'I've shown you mine, you

show me you me yours. I dare you.'

Never one to refuse a challenge, Katy put Daphne's knickers onto the bedcover and pulled up her own skirt. She saw Daphne look at her thighs admiringly as they were slowly revealed, and she realised that the dark-haired beauty fancied her.

At the thought, her cunt began to lubricate again, as if it needed to be any wetter, with the remains of her fuck puddling in her pants.

'Strawberry pink,' said Daphne admiringly as Katy exposed her undies. 'Are they part of one of the sets that Sir Charles bought you?'

Katy nodded.

What am I doing? she thought as she pulled down her knickers to expose her pubic bush, so different in colour and texture to Daphne's but equally alluring to men as she kept discovering. The inside of her knickers too, were wet with thick jism that had trickled out of her cunt, and Daphne stood up and examined it, touched the spunk with her fingers and licked it off them with her tongue. 'It's lovely and warm,' she said. 'Can I put them on?'

Katy handed her the wet knickers and Daphne gracefully stepped into them and pulled them up tightly. 'Lovely.' she said. 'Will you wear mine?'

Katy nodded, picked up Daphne's knickers from where she'd put them, daintily stepped into them and pulled them up around her hips. The mixture of Daphne's and Dave's spunk was cold on her hot pussy, but the lubrication and come that was dribbling out of it soon warmed the mess that coated Daphne's undies.

The two young women stood together, facing each other in the centre of the room and Katy could feel the sexual tension crackling through the air as if it were alive. Then Daphne moved closer and kissed Katy full on the lips, took her into her arms and they moved closer together as the kiss extended into a full embrace. Katy loved the feel of Daphne's smooth skin on hers, and the smell of perfume and sex that exuded from her body.

When they broke apart Daphne said, 'Do you want to stay the night? I get so lonely here on my own.'

'Mark . . .' said Katy.

'Give him a ring, I'm sure he won't mind. Use the phone by the bed.'

Almost mesmerised, Katy did as Daphne told her, sat on the bed, picked up the telephone receiver from its place next to one of the lamps on the bedside table and dialled cousin Mark's number. He answered on the fifth ring.

'Katy,' he said when she spoke. 'Is something wrong?'

'No,' replied Katy. 'I'm at Daphne's place in Lavender Hill. I'm tired. I think I'll stay the night. Is that alright?'

'Of course, darling.'

'I'll be home first thing,' said Katy.

Daphne sat next to Katy and signalled for her to give her the phone. 'Hello, Mark,' she said when she took it. 'Daphne here. It's my fault. I'm all alone tonight and I want Katy to keep me company. I hope you don't mind.'

Katy heard the buzz of Mark's voice at the other end of the line.

'Sure,' said Daphne. 'I'll make sure she gets a cab straight after breakfast. Don't worry. She'll be back with you by ten. Bye-bye, Mark,' and she put down the receiver.

'Didn't want him to think you were up to anything,' she said. 'Even if you are,' and she leant over and kissed Katy full on the lips again. The kiss lengthened once more, and both girls opened their mouths and began to explore each other with their tongues. Once again Katy marvelled at the smooth feel of Daphne's skin on hers, the scent of her perfume and the softness of her breasts as they pushed against Katy's own.

Daphne's hands roamed over Katy's body, setting fire to the nerve ends as they went. Katy had never been kissed and caressed by a woman before, and she found herself not only enjoying the experience, but wanting to kiss and caress Daphne back.

The older woman lay Katy back on the bed and ran her hands up under her skirt to her naked thighs, between her stockings and the panties that she had been wearing herself up until a few minutes before.

Daphne's roving hands pushed Katy's legs apart and went straight to the centre of her womanhood and rubbed the come-soaked material into the slit between Katy's thighs.

'Is that nice?' whispered Daphne.

'Wonderful.'

'Did Kenny make you come?'

Katy nodded.

'Dave made me come too. That means you've got four comes in your cunt now.'

'It feels lovely,' said Katy.

'Rub mine,' said Daphne. 'I want four too.'

Katy did as she was told. As Daphne pulled her own skirt up around her waist and opened her beautiful, long, slim legs wide Katy put her hand down between Daphne's thighs and touched her own panties, now worn by her darkhaired seductress, and rubbed at the hairiness of her quim through the sopping material. Daphne closed her eyes in enjoyment as Katy's red-tipped fingers found her pussy opening through the flimsy material and pushed it up her love tunnel.

'Take them off and snog me there,' said Daphne. 'I want to feel your tongue up me drinking out our love juices.'

Katy didn't need telling twice. She got off the bed, knelt on the floor and pulled the strawberry-pink panties that Daphne was wearing off her hips and down her legs. Then she attached her mouth to the hairy lips of Daphne's cunt and kissed it passionately, licking her clitoris and sucking the combined love juice of four people from the membranes of Daphne's quim and down her throat like a woman who'd been dying of thirst and had found a well of pure sweet spring water.

Katy loved the feel of Daphne's hairy minge in her mouth as much as she'd enjoyed kissing Sir Charles's moustachioed lips. As she knelt between her friend's legs, lapping at her pussy, she thought in wonderment about the beautiful sex that she'd experienced since coming up to London as a virgin, just a few short weeks before, to meet Mark and attend her first job interview.

31

After Katy had been eating Daphne's peach for a few minutes, and her face was covered in two men's and two women's come, Daphne caught her hair in her hands and gently pulled her up to lie next to her on the bed again. 'Strip me,' she said. 'Make me naked.'

Katy did as her new lover told her, gently unbuttoning, unzipping and unfastening her clothes, tossing them across the top of the bed until Daphne was naked before her.

'You're beautiful,' whispered Katy. 'Strip *me* now.'

Daphne repaid the compliment, and within a few minutes both women were naked.

Daphne pulled back the covers of the bed and they lay together on the crisp, clean bottom sheet with their heads resting on the pillows, gazing into each other's eyes.

'I've never made love to a woman before,' said Katy.

'I guessed you hadn't,' said Daphne. 'It's wonderful. But sometimes you need some help.'

'What kind of help?'

'I'll show you,' said Daphne, and rolled off the bed and went over to the wardrobe, opened the door, pulled down a box, carried it back to the bed and opened the lid. She pulled out a vibrator and a huge black leather dildo with thick straps. She switched on the vibrator, which hummed busily, and she smiled. 'I love this one,' she said. 'It makes me go tingly all over. Have you ever used one?'

'No,' said Katy.

'You've got a treat in store then.'

Daphne placed the vibrator between Katy's legs and the young blonde felt it throb across her pubic bone, and the most delightful sensations swept through her body.

'That's *gorgeous*,' she said. 'Oh, I love it.'

'I've got lots of toys in my box,' said Daphne. 'We're going to have fun trying them all out,' and she slid the tip of the vibrator into Katy's wet and open cunt, and began to push it up her tunnel of love.

The further she pushed it, the better it felt to Katy, and she opened her legs wide to allow the plastic knob easier access.

When Katy felt she was full to the brim, and the vibrator was almost completely inside her, Daphne left it in her cunt with the motor running and began to knead her breasts, pinching the nipples up hard and kissing Katy's face and neck, licking off the come that was drying on her skin.

Katy responded with kisses of her own, feeling the mechanical penis rumbling deep inside her and sending waves of pleasure, the like of which she'd never experienced before, to the pleasure centres of her brain. She closed her legs tightly around it so as not to miss any of the delights she could feel.

'I'm going to come,' she cried as her whole body throbbed to the beat of the electric motor of the vibrator. 'I am. Daphne, hold me tight.'

Daphne did as she pleaded, and Katy's whole being seemed to fill with joy and she pulled Daphne towards her. Their mouths met in a long lingering snog as she came again and again onto the hard plastic of the sex machine filling her pussy.

32

Katy collapsed back in a sweaty heap and Daphne pulled the vibrator, inch by inch, out of her cunt. 'I want you to fuck me now,' she said.

'How?' asked Katy.

'With the leather strap-on.'

'How does it work?' Katy was intrigued.

'It gives us both a thrill. I'll show you.'

Daphne picked up the huge black leather dildo and got Katy to kneel on the bed with her legs apart. She fastened one strap around Katy's waist, then fed the other between her legs and up the crack in her arse and buckled that one too, so that the strap bit into the sensitive wetness between her legs and the dildo stuck out obscenely from her groin like an erect penis.

'There you go,' said Daphne. 'How does that feel?'

'Great,' replied Katy. 'It's rubbing my clit.'

'That's perfect then. Now screw me.'

'How?'

'You are silly, Katy,' said Daphne, lying on the bed, legs wide and her sex peeping through her black pubes. 'Just like Kenny fucked you.'

Katy lay between Daphne's legs and Daphne found the end of the dildo and guided it into her pink gash.

'Push it in,' she said. 'Not too hard.'

Katy did as she was told and Daphne's face filled with pleasure, her mouth opened and as Katy lay on top of her they kissed.

'Move it in and out.'

Once again Katy did as she was told. The feeling between her legs as the leather strap rubbed on her clitoris was wonderful, and she could tell that Daphne was enjoying being invaded by the dildo; she moaned and panted under Katy's body, the two women's breasts rubbing together, their four nipples as big and hard as acorns.

'Faster,' urged Daphne. 'Fuck me harder.'

'I don't want to hurt you.'

'You won't. But I don't care if you do. Screw me harder.'

Katy increased the speed of her thrusts into Daphne's pussy, and the faster she went, the better her cunt felt, as the hard leather strap opened her pussy up wide and pushed the lips of her crack further apart.

Daphne put her legs around Katy's back and pulled her closer, and their bodies stuck slickly together with the juices from their night of sex and the sweat that sprung from their pores and trickled down between them.

'I'm going to come,' screamed Daphne. 'Fuck me harder. Beat me. Punish me. Fuck me you little bitch. Your dirty little dyke. You tart. You whore.'

Katy loved being called filthy names by her girl-friend, and pumped the dildo harder in the hole between Daphne's legs, until the dark-haired girl screamed and mashed her mouth against Katy's, and the young blonde tasted blood in her mouth as Daphne's teeth broke the skin of her bottom lip.

After Daphne's orgasm, they rolled over together, and lay facing one another, still joined by the obscene instrument strapped over Katy's hips.

'Great,' said Daphne. 'No man's ever fucked me better. You've got a lot of potential, Katy.'

'Thank you,' said Katy, withdrawing the hard leather sex toy from Daphne's quim.

'Do you want for us to come together?' asked Daphne.

'Aren't you tired yet?' asked Katy.

'Just one more, then we can go to sleep. Please?' said the dark-haired girl.

'OK,' said Katy. 'Just one more.'

Daphne returned to her box of tricks and withdrew another dildo. This time it was made of soft, foam rubber and was double-ended. She knelt on the bed and inserted one of the ends into her gash, then told Katy to kneel facing her and push the other end into her own pussy, until they were locked together with their pubic bushes and clitorises rubbing against each other's.

Slowly they started to move their hips together, feeling their pubic mounds bumping and grinding, until they settled into a steady rhythm and their cunts rotated gently together sending wonderful messages of delight through their bodies. They embraced, and their breasts rubbed together too, and then as they moved they plastered their mouths together in a long delightful kiss.

Katy was the first of the pair to come. She felt her orgasm building inside her loins as Daphne's thick, crinkly pubes ground into the softness of her own blonde hair and her clitoris banged onto her bi-sexual friend's pudenda.

She pulled her mouth away from Daphne's hungry lips and gasped, 'I'm coming,' and moved one hand down to the twin globes of Daphne's arse and pulled her closer so that their thighs rubbed together. It would have been impossible to insert a single sheet of paper between their sweaty bodies.

'Wait,' cried Daphne. 'Wait, you cunt. Don't you dare come without me.'

'I can't help it,' panted Katy. 'I can't help it.'

Daphne pulled one hand back and slapped Katy in the face hard. The blow felt like a kiss to the young blonde, but it had the required effect of slowing her orgasm for a moment, until Daphne screamed that she was coming too, and the pair of them sobbed in mutual delight as their twin comes burst through their bodies at precisely the same moment, and they collapsed together on the damp sheet.

'Did I hurt you, darling?' cooed Daphne, and she kissed Katy's cheek where the red imprint of her fingers was clearly to be seen.

'No,' said Katy. 'It felt lovely.'

'Then one day I'm going to tie you up and whip you,' said Daphne.

'That sounds delicious. But not now,' pleaded Katy, who was suddenly overcome with a vast weariness following her sexual activities first with Kenny and now her unexpected initiation into lesbian love by Daphne.

'No, darling, not now,' whispered Daphne. 'You go to sleep now, and I'll hold you all night long.'

33

Katy woke up at eight-fifteen when Daphne kissed her forehead. The brunette was standing next to the bed, dressed in a red silk kimono and holding a cup and saucer.

'Tea?' she said.

For a minute Katy didn't know where she was, or why. Then the events of the previous night rushed back and she blushed. 'Daphne,' she said, 'Did we . . .?'

Daphne nodded and smiled. 'Yes, we did,' she said. 'Any regrets?'

Katy shook her head. 'No,' she said, 'no regrets,' and sat up, exposing her naked breasts to the lustful eyes of her lesbian lover. As she did so, she felt a stab of delicious pain between her legs. 'Oh,' she said. 'My cunt's sore.'

'Too much fucking,' said Daphne. 'Now, do you want this tea or not?'

'Please. My mouth tastes awful.'

'Too much champagne,' said Daphne, handed her the cup and saucer, shucked off her kimono to expose her naked body beneath and joined Katy in bed.

The two women lay next to each other as Katy

drank the tea, Daphne's hand just touching her thigh.

When the cup was empty, Katy put it and the saucer on the bedside table and rolled over to face Daphne. 'Can we do it again?' she asked.

'You'll be late home,' teased Daphne.

'Mark can wait,' said Katy. 'We can go food shopping later.'

'Ah, domestic bliss,' said Daphne.

'What time is your husband due back?'

'This afternoon. But don't worry. Even if he came in now, he'd only want to watch.'

'Has he watched you before?'

'Sure.'

'With other girls?'

'And my boyfriends. It turns him on. It's the only way I can get him really horny.'

'Would you like him to watch us?' asked Katy.

'Would *you*?'

'I wouldn't mind.'

'He'd probably want to join in. Would you mind that?'

Katy shook her head.

'You're a filthy little bitch, Katy,' said Daphne. 'But he's alright. Got quite a nice bod and a big dick. And when he gets excited he's quite athletic. He just likes different things, that's all.'

'Like watching.' said Katy.

'Like watching,' agreed Daphne.

'Whatever turns you on,' said Katy.

'Kissing your cunt turns me on,' said Daphne.

'So do it then.'

Daphne slid down the length of the bed and placed her mouth over Katy's cunt. Daphne thought it was the sweetest taste she'd ever known as she licked and poked her tongue up into the wet heat of Katy's pussy.

Katy shivered and shook as Daphne's tongue snaked into her private parts. And as her lover's long, dark hair caressed the tops of her thighs and her belly, all thoughts of the pain from the rough usage of her delicate pussy vanished. Daphne moved round so that she could get her tongue deeper between Katy's legs, which Katy opened as wide as they would go. Katy hoped that the delicious feeling that was working its way through her body would never end.

Daphne rolled her over and pulled the cheeks of her arse apart, licked down the crack and poked the tip of her tongue into Katy's anus. Katy bit down on the pillow to stop herself screaming with delight.

Daphne opened up Katy's wet arsehole with her little finger, then gently pushed it inside, and Katy could no longer contain herself and had her first orgasm of the day as she felt Daphne push the finger inside her right up to the first knuckle.

When she'd stopped shaking from the force of her come, Daphne withdrew her finger and Katy rolled over onto her back, and Daphne mounted her and they kissed.

'That was wonderful,' said Katy, after they broke away from each other. 'I'm still trembling.'

'I'm going to show you so much,' said Daphne. 'All the wonderful things we can do to each other.'

'I can't wait,' said Katy.

"Make me come before you go,' said Daphne. 'Wank me off.'

Katy put her hand down between their two bodies and found Daphne's open cunt, the lubrication

187

dribbling out making it easier for her to open the lips and find Daphne's clit. She started to rub her there with gentle circling movements.

Daphne shivered as Katy's fingers found her most delicate parts, and she kissed and bit at the young blonde's neck as she writhed on top of Katy's supine form, increasingly desperate as she felt Katy's fingers moving faster inside the rich wetness of her pussy.

'Harder,' she cried. 'Hurt me.'

Katy pinched Daphne's clitoris cruelly, and the brunette shrieked with pleasure until she could stand it no longer and she orgasmed her rich juices onto Katy's hand.

They lay together for another few minutes until Katy whispered, 'I'd better get dressed.'

'Don't go,' said Daphne.

'I have to.'

'I don't want you to.'

'And I don't want to go, but I must.'

'You're cruel.'

'I'll see you on Monday.'

'It won't be the same.'

'It will. You wait and see.'

'Promise.'

'Of course,' said Katy.

'Can we sleep together again?'

'You bet.'

'I love you,' said Daphne.

'And I love you too,' replied Katy.

34

Katy got home around eleven that morning, after showering the stink of sweat and sex off her body with Daphne, in the tiny shower stall at her flat, which ended in them having more steamy sex on the bathroom floor. After that she got dressed in last night's soiled clothing, with the only change being the loan of a pair of Daphne's clean knickers to replace Katy's own, which were wet with come.

'I'll bring them to work on Monday, and give you them back then,' she told her lover.

'Don't wash them', said Daphne. 'I want to wear them for a bit myself first.'

'You're filthy,' said Katy as she kissed her friend on the mouth, and went outside to the Wandsworth Road to hail a cab to take her back to Waterloo.

Mark was sitting at the dining table, fully dressed and drinking coffee when she arrived. 'Sorry I'm later than I thought, love,' she said as she entered and kissed him on the cheek. 'Daphne and I got nattering last night, and I didn't get to sleep till four.'

'Girls night out, was it?' asked Mark.

'You can say that again.'

'What's Daphne like?'

'Terrific. We're thinking of making it a regular Friday night thing, OK?'

'Fine by me. You should get out with more people your own age.'

'Hark at Grandad.'

Mark smiled, and Katy felt only a tiny twinge of conscience at her recent unfaithfulness. What the eye doesn't see, the heart doesn't grieve over, she thought.

'So what's on the agenda today?' she asked, pouring herself a cup of coffee from the pot.

'Shopping. Lunch. Maybe a film.'

'Sounds good. Let me go and change. I've still got my office stuff on. Then we'll go.'

She was barely five minutes getting changed, stuffing her dirty undies, including Daphne's knickers, well down into the laundry basket and slipping into a sweater and jeans before returning to the living room where Mark was waiting.

'Are you fit?' he asked.

She nodded, and hand in hand they left the flat in the direction of the supermarket, which was close to the riverside.

On the way back, laden down with the week's shopping, they stopped for a drink in a bar that cousin Mark knew well. 'Where for lunch?' he asked.

'The Italian,' said Katy. 'I'm starving.'

'Sounds good,' said Mark. 'We'll just have another here, then we'll be off.'

Lunch was indeed good, the couple being warmly greeted and placed at the best table in the place. When they were on their coffee Mark said, 'A film?'

'I don't think so,' said Katy. 'I'm still a bit tired. I'd like a lazy afternoon back at the flat with the TV on.'

'Suits me,' said her cousin. 'We've got a couple of bottles of wine in the bags. We'll make an evening of it. Call out for Chinese or something.'

'Lovely,' said Katy.

They walked back to the flat weighed down with their purchases and straight up to the kitchen where they shoved them into the cupboards and the fridge. 'Better make it red to start,' said Mark. 'Give the white time to cool down.'

'Sounds fine,' said Katy. 'I'll be in the sitting room.'

She went through, kicked off her shoes, switched on the TV, found an old black and white film and dropped onto the sofa. God, I'm tired, she thought, and my cunt still aches from all the punishment it took last night. I wonder if Mark wants to . . .

As if on cue he came into the room with the opened bottle of wine and two glasses which he set on the coffee table in front of the sofa. 'Budge up,' he said, and Katy moved her legs and he sat next to her.

He poured out the wine and they toasted each other. 'Thanks for a lovely lunch,' said Katy, and leant over to kiss him on the cheek, but he moved his face and caught her mouth on his.

Yes, he does, she thought. Oh well, in for a penny.

Mark put down his glass and took Katy's from her and placed it next to his own, then gathered her up in his arms and kissed her more passionately on the lips. Immediately, almost despite herself, she began to respond. Christ, she thought, I'm getting to be such a horny bitch, and moved her legs round so that she trapped Mark's body between them and could rub her cunt up against his hips. The kiss extended as their mouths opened and their tongues met in a puddle of

191

sticky spit and Katy bit down hard on Mark's lower lip until he pulled his face away from her's. 'You're passionate,' he said.

'I haven't had it for ages,' she whispered demurely. 'I'm horny.'

'Let's go to bed.'

'No. Let's do it here on the carpet.'

'Whatever turns you on.'

'You do,' and they tumbled together to the floor and started tearing each other's clothes off.

Katy was the first one naked, her jeans, socks, sweater, knickers and bra strewn across the floor, then she ripped Mark's shirt off his back, losing a couple of buttons as she did so, then *his* jeans and his underpants, to allow her access to his long, swollen prick which she took in her hand then into her mouth.

As she went down on him, she stuck her bottom into the air so that he could finger her damp pussy and rub the slime up her crack to lubricate the opening of her arsehole. She'd learnt that she loved fingers and cocks being pushed into her anus, and that butt-fucking was as much, if not more, pleasurable than being poked in her pussy.

Mark knew exactly what she wanted, inserted two fingers into her cunt from behind, scooped up as much of her juices as he could, and gently inserted one finger into her back passage.

Katy wriggled luxuriously as his finger slid up her, and she sucked harder at his cock, sliding her tongue over the hardness of his helmet and inserted the tip of her tongue into the hole.

Mark gasped as the sensation shot through his body and he wiggled his finger harder in her arse, opening it wider so that he could get a second finger into the darkness there.

Katy moved her face off his groin and looked over her shoulder. 'Fuck me there,' she said. 'Put your cock in my arse.'

Mark grinned, pulled his fingers out, lay her face down on the carpet, opened her legs and climbed onto her back. He found more lubrication in her pussy and smeared it down his cock, then pushed the tip between the cheeks of her bottom and found her hole. Gently he pushed the end of his knob into her anus. Katy stiffened as she felt the pain at first but, then, once more it turned to pleasure as his prick pushed deeper into her, until it was all the way in and Mark started to fuck his young lover.

Gently he eased his tool in and out of her orifice, building up the friction until she thought she'd die from the wonderful feeling that filled her.

'Faster,' she cried. 'Faster.'

He did as she said, building up the power of his thrusts until he jetted his hot spunk inside her and collapsed on top of her prone body.

'Oh Mark,' she said after a moment. 'That felt so good. Make me come now. Do it with your mouth.'

Mark lifted himself gently off her and his softening cock left her body with a wet plop, then he rolled her over and went down on her bush with his face.

His questing tongue found her cunt, and he pushed it into the sweet liquid that bubbled out and dribbled down the insides of her thighs, drinking it down like the wine that they'd abandoned in the glasses beside where they were making love.

Katy lifted those beautiful thighs and trapped his

head between them so that he couldn't escape until he'd given her the pleasure she craved, and as she tightened their grip, he lapped at her all the harder, finding her clitoris with his teeth and nibbling at the tiny organ.

Mark's tongue felt so good inside her, soothing the slight pain she still felt up in her cunt, that the familiar warm feeling soon permeated every nerve in her body. She gave herself completely to the sensation and came into his mouth with a sob of delight.

35

Katy was back at her desk as usual on Monday morning with the coffee pot gently burbling on its hot plate, and a fresh pint of milk in the fridge, when Sir Charles came through the door.

'Good morning, Miss Dunn,' he said. 'I trust you had a good weekend.'

'Very good thank you,' replied Katy.

'I'll have my coffee now, then I wish to speak with you about a very important matter.'

Intrigued, Katy did her chores, then when Sir Charles buzzed through on the intercom, she went into his office where he was waiting for her on the sofa. He patted the cushion next to him and she sat down, demurely crossing her legs.

'Next weekend,' he said. 'Are you busy?'

'Not particularly,' said Katy.

'I have to go to France next Monday, and there's a conference in Canterbury at the end of this week. I need some notes brought back. I wonder if you'd mind coming down to Folkestone on Friday and spending the weekend there with me, then returning to London on Sunday with the papers.'

Katy was stunned. 'Folkestone. I don't know,' she stammered.

'It's not the most romantic of settings, I know,' said Sir Charles. 'But I'll book us into a discreet and comfortable hotel. We could have fun.'

'I'll have to think about it. There's my boyfriend to consider.'

Sir Charles smiled. 'I haven't noticed you giving him much consideration lately.'

Little do you know, thought Katy.

'It'll be strictly business as far as he's concerned. And no one here need know anything about it. As far as they're aware, the papers will have been delivered to you by messenger on Monday.' When he saw that Katy was still undecided, he added, 'I promise that you'll get the best of everything. I'll even book the honeymoon suite.'

Katy hesitated. The honeymoon suite, she thought. Just what I want. 'Alright, Sir Charles,' she said. 'I'll come.'

'Good,' said Sir Charles. 'I'll make all the arrangements. All you have to do is meet me at Folkestone Station on Friday afternoon. I'll arrange with personnel that you have the afternoon off. Your first-class ticket will be here tomorrow. Now how about a taste of what we're going to do all weekend?'

Why not? thought Katy, as Sir Charles pulled her close and kissed her. Everybody else I've met has.

Katy sucked at Sir Charles's tongue as his hands roamed over the jacket of her tailored suit and pushed it off her shoulders. Then one hand found her brassiered breast through the thin cotton of her blouse and the other explored under the hem of her skirt and pushed up between her thighs, to the smooth naked flesh above her stocking tops, and then further to the tight bundle of her crotch where he could feel her crinkly pubic hair through the thin material of her panties.

At his touch, Katy's cunt opened and she began to lubricate, and as he probed her pants with his fingers, he felt the dampness soak through them. He pushed her skirt up so that he could see the sheer white silk was transparent and exposed the pink lips of her pussy to his lustful eyes.

'Beautiful,' breathed Sir Charles, and sank to his knees before her, and attached his lips to the lips of her cunt through her knickers.

Katy hauled her skirt higher, opened her legs and lay back on the leather sofa with her eyes closed in sheer bliss as Sir Charles's mouth worked on her through the fine, wet silk of her panties. When he was tired of that, he pushed the gusset to one side and re-attached his mouth to the nakedness of her pussy, tonguing and biting at the hole until she could hardly bear it.

She reached down and pushed his head harder against her hole, and she felt his moustache tickle at the delicate skin inside it, and at that feeling, much to her amazement and delight, she came.

'Did you enjoy that, my dear?' asked Sir Charles, pulling his face away from her fragrant minge. 'I believe you did.'

'It was your moustache,' she panted. 'Inside me. I couldn't hold back.'

'And nor should you. Take your pleasure where you can, and as often as possible. That's what I always say.'

Sir Charles rose from his knees and started to

undress, and Katy struggled out of her clothes, still sitting on the sofa, until they were both naked and the carpet and furniture were draped with their garments.

'And now it's my turn for pleasure,' said Sir Charles as he lowered himself between Katy's legs whilst she stretched on the length of the sofa, one of her feet on the carpet, the other on the back of the seat, with her head resting on the arm of it.

Sir Charles's long, hard knob immediately found the entrance to her private parts and easily pushed down into the hot, open wetness of her love tunnel until his balls slid into the crack between her buttocks. Katy hugged his body close to hers, and they began the age-old movements of love once more.

They now knew each other well enough so that each was aware of what the other desired from fucking. Katy scratched the skin of Sir Charles's back just hard enough to tingle, and he slid his hand under her bottom until one finger could tickle gently at the puckered hole there.

Faster and faster they moved together, Katy hooking her ankles over Sir Charles's calves and mashing her lips on his, their tongues and teeth working together for maximum pleasure and their bodies so close together that she felt that they might melt into one single being.

Finally, when she thought Sir Charles could screw her no harder, he found one last burst of energy and she clung on to him for dear life as he pounded her almost through the seats of the sofa then stopped dead; she felt his hot juices burst inside her body and fill her to the brim with his come.

'Christ,' he cried. 'That was magnificent, you young whore.'

'I am your whore,' said Katy. 'And I always will be.'

'Yes, you will,' he said as he withdrew. 'Now get dressed, I've got a meeting before lunch, and I don't want to be late.'

Katy did as she was told, and after Sir Charles had left the office she called down to the typing pool and asked to speak to Daphne.

'Hello,' said her friend when she came on the line. 'How are *you*?'

'Never better,' said Katy. 'Lunch?'

'I'm on earlies,' replied Daphne. 'Twelve o'clock.'

'Doesn't matter. Sir Charles has gone out. I'll meet you in the pub at five past.'

Katy was standing at the bar when Daphne arrived, and when they both had drinks they found a table and went up to the food service area and ordered a salad each. When they were back at their seats, Daphne said, 'Did you bring my knickers with you?'

'Yes,' said Katy. 'They're in my bag.'

'Give them to me.'

'What, here?'

'Yes.'

Katy reached into her handbag and retrieved the delicate garment, folded them tightly and passed them to her lesbian lover, who put them to her face and breathed their perfume in deeply. 'You haven't washed them?'

'I told you I wouldn't.'

'They smell lovely. Just like your cunt.'

Katy blushed.

'Did you enjoy yourself on Friday night?' asked Daphne.

'I should say so,' replied Katy. 'Did you?'

'It was the best night I've had for years. Shall we do it again next week?'

'I can't on Friday,' said Katy sadly, and explained why.

'A weekend away with Sir Charles,' said Daphne. 'You are the lucky one. Shall we make it another night then?'

Katy nodded.

'Come round for dinner on Wednesday. Bob will be there.' Bob was Daphne's husband. 'We could have fun.'

'I'd like that,' said Katy, feeling the mixture of her own and Sir Charles's come between her legs, and wanting more sex, there and then. 'I'd like that very much. About as much as I'd like to fuck you now with that leather dildo, right across the table here.'

'In front of all these people?'

Katy nodded.

'I wish you could. But have patience, wait till Wednesday night, there's no knowing what might happen.'

'I know what I want to happen,' said Katy.

'So it's a date,' said Daphne.

Katy nodded.

'What are you going to tell Mark that you're doing at the weekend?'

'I'll tell him the truth. That I'm going away on business.'

'Funny business,' said Daphne, and both the girls

laughed. 'You are a naughty girl, Katy,' she went on.

'Only you know just how naughty,' replied the young blonde.

'And it's our secret. At least until Wednesday. After that who knows?'

'Who knows indeed?' replied Katy.

36

On Wednesday evening Katy met Daphne at the main doors of the office building. She'd told Mark about her weekend away on business, and although he wasn't best pleased at being left alone he knew that as secretary to a director there would be times when she'd have to work unusual hours. When he'd said that, she'd thought that she'd have to work unusual positions too, but said nothing, and hid the smile that came to her lips.

He wasn't too pleased either when she'd told him that because she'd be away on Friday evening she'd decided to have her 'Girls night out' as she called it on Wednesday. But after some kissing and canoodling he'd come round.

Men are so easy, thought Katy when he did. A bit of tit and thigh and they'll agree to anything. If anyone had told her she was getting cynical she probably wouldn't have known what they were talking about.

She and Daphne went straight to the pub for a quick drink before heading towards Daphne's place, dinner, and Katy didn't know what else next, although she had an idea. An idea that thrilled her from the toes of her sheer nylons to the tips of her carefully arranged blonde hair.

'You look lovely tonight, Katy,' said Daphne, when they were seated at a table in the bar, with a gin and tonic each.

'Thank you,' said Katy in reply. 'You don't look too bad yourself.'

Daphne smiled. 'Bob's getting supper ready,' she said. 'He's dying to meet you.'

'Does he know what we did on Friday?' asked Katy.

'He guessed.'

'Does he mind?'

Daphne shook her head of lustrous, dark hair. 'No. Not at all. Like I said he can't wait to meet you.'

'Fair enough,' said Katy. 'I'm looking forward to meeting him too.'

'Just don't give him too much attention, or you'll make me jealous,' said Daphne.

'I wouldn't want to do that,' replied Katy, lowering her eyelashes demurely. 'Have you washed your knickers yet?'

'No. I wore them last night in bed. Bob got quite amorous. I told him where they'd been and he couldn't wait to get them off me.'

'You didn't,' said Katy. 'I thought you hadn't told him about us.'

'I didn't. Not until he worked it out for himself. I was talking about you all weekend, and what a good time we had on Friday.'

'Did you tell him about Kenny and Dave?'

'Only when we were fucking.'

'Did he mind about you screwing Dave?'

'No. He was only sorry about not being there to

see it. I told you he was kinky.'

'He must be.'

'What would Mark say about you and Kenny, or Sir Charles, or me?'

'God knows? I think he'd be furious.'

'Don't tell him then.'

'I won't unless I have to.'

'Why would you have to?'

'Who knows? If I wanted to split up from him, I suppose.'

'Split up, you've only been together for a few weeks.'

'But there might be more interesting fish in the sea.'

Daphne looked surprised. 'Like who?'

'Like Sir Charles Wheeler.'

'*Sir Charles*.'

'That's right. I intend to marry him.'

'Are you joking? No one's ever been able to tie that old devil down. He's a confirmed bachelor.'

'Anyone can change.'

'Not that old devil.'

'Don't you believe it, Daphne,' said Katy. 'I think I can hook him, and if I can, I will.'

'Well, good luck, girl, many have tried before you, and many have failed.'

'We'll see,' said Katy, and raised her glass to Daphne in a toast. 'Are we going soon? I'm getting hungry.'

It was seven o'clock so the pair of them caught a cab down to Daphne's place. She let them through the front door; the flat was warm and smelled deliciously of spicy cooking, and Daphne said, 'He's a good cook.'

'Sure smells like it,' said Katy. 'What's on the menu tonight?'

'Just wait and see,' said Daphne with a smile.

She dragged Katy into the kitchen where a good-looking man was hunched over pots at the stove. He straightened up at their entrance and Daphne said, 'Bob, this Katy. Katy, Bob.'

Katy was surprised at how handsome Daphne's husband was. He stood about six-foot two in his polished loafers and he wore tight blue jeans and a white denim shirt. His hair was brown and thick, and he smiled at the two girls as he walked over towards them 'Katy,' he said, 'I've heard a lot about you. Welcome.'

'Thanks, Bob,' she said. 'I've heard a lot about you too. What are you cooking? It certainly smells good.'

'My speciality. Chicken in tomato sauce with peppers and onions, and new potatoes with fresh peas.'

'Great,' said Katy. 'I'm starving.'

'That's what I wanted to hear,' said Bob. 'I like a girl with a good appetite. You two go in the other room. I'll bring in some wine and we'll eat in about twenty minutes. Is that OK?'

'Sounds fine,' said Daphne. 'Come on, Katy. We're going to be waited on tonight for a change.'

Katy and Daphne went into the living room, where the dining table had been set for three on a gleaming white cloth. Bob followed them a moment later carrying a bottle of red and a bottle of white wine. 'I didn't know which you preferred, Katy,' he said. 'So I brought both.'

'The white looks good,' said Katy.

'White it is then,' said Bob, putting the bottle of red in the centre of the table. He picked up an opener and expertly opened the bottle of white wine, and poured out three glasses.

The dinner was delicious, and the wine flowed freely

throughout. When Bob brought in the coffee after-wards, he also produced a bottle of brandy with which he liberally filled three glasses so many times that Katy quite lost count of how much she'd drunk.

After the dishes were cleared away, Daphne went to the stereo and put on a CD by Whitney Houston then sat down on the sofa next to Katy. As she sat her skirt rode up her thighs to expose her stocking tops, suspenders and the bare skin of her legs, but she ignored the fact and made no effort to pull it down. 'Do you like Whitney?' she asked, and her words were slightly slurred.

'Yes,' said Katy. 'She's one of my favourites. I've got all her albums at home.'

'Very romantic,' said Daphne. 'Bob loves her.'

'She is good,' agreed Bob. 'Just the thing to listen to after an excellent dinner with two beautiful women.'

'You silver-tongued devil,' said Daphne. 'Let's dance. I feel like dancing.'

Bob got to his feet and pulled Daphne to hers, and they began to dance to a slow track on the album. They stood very close, embracing and hardly moving their feet to the music, just rubbing their groins together to the beat.

'Don't you want to dance with my handsome hus-band?' Daphne asked Katy. 'He can really move.'

'I'd love to,' said Katy, and climbed to her feet herself, and went over to Bob as Daphne slid out of his embrace, threw herself back onto the sofa and poured another glass of brandy.

The track on the record ended, and as another slow ballad began, Bob took Katy into his arms and they began to dance.

He was indeed a good dancer and Katy felt quite at home as they moved round the centre of the room. As she looked up into his eyes he pulled her closer to his body until their groins met and she could feel the lump of his manhood in his trousers against her lower belly.

'So what were you two little dears getting up to the other night?' he said. 'When I was away earning the mortgage on this place.'

Katy felt herself blush under the scrutiny of his dark eyes and replied, 'We just went out for a few drinks,' and she heard Daphne giggle from her perch on the far side of the room.

'That's not what I heard,' said Bob. 'I heard the pair of you were quite naughty,' and he pulled Katy even closer and she felt his prick stiffen in his pants as he pushed it against her.

'Not *too* naughty,' she said and pushed back against his knob with the roundness of her belly.

Bob smiled. 'But how naughty is not too naughty?' he asked.

'I thought Daphne had told you.'

'She has, but I want you to tell me too.'

'I couldn't,' said Katy.

'Go on,' said Daphne from her seat. 'Tell him. He's dying to hear.'

'OK,' said Katy, deciding to bluff it out. 'We slept with a couple of guys then went to bed together and made love.'

She felt Bob's cock rear up even harder at her words and knew that, between them, she and Daphne could twist him round their little fingers, and she turned and winked at her dark-haired friend who smiled back and licked her lips lasciviously.

As the music ended Bob grabbed Katy by the wrist and led her back to the sofa where she sat next to Daphne and he took a seat in one of the armchairs opposite and said, 'I want to hear every detail. Come on Katy, tell me. Show me.'

'We can't show you what we did to the guys,' said Daphne, tipsily. 'But we can show you what we did to each other, can't we, Katy?'

'Yes,' replied Katy, equally under the influence of the alcohol she'd drunk. 'Go and get your box.'

Daphne jumped to her feet and ran out of the room and upstairs to the bedroom. Bob said to Katy, 'Who led who astray?'

'It was six of one and half a dozen of the other,' she replied. 'Don't you really mind what Daphne gets up to with other people?'

'I love it,' he said back. 'I love to see the one I love having sexual pleasure with other partners. It really turns me on.'

'Then you are unusual,' said Katy.

'Not as unusual as you might think,' said Bob with a grin.

After a few minutes they both heard Daphne's feet on the stairs and she entered the room wearing only her stockings, suspenders and high-heeled shoes, with the leather dildo that she and Katy had used to such great effect on the previous Friday strapped between her legs and jutting out obscenely from her bush of black pubic hair. Under one arm she carried her box of tricks which she dropped onto the floor, then she posed in the doorway, pushing out her hips and putting one hand behind her head. 'Like it?' she said, and both Bob and Katy applauded as she walked across the carpet, swinging her backside, her full breasts with nipples erect, jiggling as she came.

'Get naked, Katy,' she said. 'I want to fuck you. It's your turn to take Black Betty up your cunt.'

With trembling hands Katy did as she was told, stripping off her clothes under the hot eyes of Daphne and her perverted husband.

When she finally removed her knickers and stood nude, she saw that Bob had undone his flies and allowed his hard knob the freedom to grow to its quite extraordinary length.

'Don't look at him,' ordered Daphne. 'You can try that one for size later. Right now I'm going to stick this little beauty I've got between *my* legs inside you and see how you like it. Kneel down on the sofa.'

Once again Katy did as she was told, and Daphne climbed onto the seat behind her and put her hand between Katy's thighs and into the hot, wet, sweet slit that had opened there, scooped out a handful of Katy's juice and smeared it up the length of the dildo for easier entry.

Katy opened her legs and felt the hard tip of the Black Betty poking at the entrance to her pussy. It felt cold and hard and sent a shiver through her body, but it was a shiver of anticipation rather than fear, as the huge head of the thing opened her cunt and began its long entry up her love tunnel. Wider and wider it forced her as it slid up inside, towards her welcoming womb, and she felt Daphne's hot breath on her back as she moved closer.

When the dildo was in as far as it would go, and Katy could feel the buckles and straps caressing her thighs, Daphne lifted one hand and cupped her breast and started to move the leather weapon in and out of Katy's delicious hole. It felt wonderful to the young blonde, and she moved with Daphne, loving every stroke of the slick leather inside her puss.

Daphne kissed and licked her neck and back and teased her tit, pinching the nipple until Katy almost cried out at the mixture of pleasure and pain that she was feeling.

'Is that good?' Daphne asked breathlessly. 'Tell us that it's good.'

'It is,' gasped Katy. 'It's wonderful. Fuck me harder. Make me come.'

'You'll come when I tell you, you little bitch,' said Daphne, and fucked Katy harder, until she could hardly bear it.

Then Daphne stopped and withdrew the dildo.

'No,' cried Katy. 'Don't stop.'

'Turn round, lie down,' ordered the dark-haired lesbian. 'I want to look in your eyes as you come.'

Katy slithered round on the sofa quickly and lay on her back with her legs open wide, knowing that Bob was staring at her wet, pink, open cunt, and loving the feeling of his eyes on her.

Daphne lay on top of Katy's body and expertly guided her leather tool in between the blonde's legs, again in the missionary position. She lay flat on top of Katy, her nylon stockings rasping on Katy's bare legs, and kissed her as she started to move again. The kiss lasted for as long as it took to bring Katy to orgasm, which was only a few seconds, as the feeling of the huge, hard dildo coming at her from a different angle drove her almost to distraction and made her come almost immediately, her wanton cries muffled by Daphne's mouth covering hers.

The two women lay together, breathing heavily after their sexual encounter and, slowly, Daphne withdrew the dildo from Katy's hot and succulent pussy.

'Was that good for you, darling?' the dark-haired beauty whispered.

'Beautiful,' said Katy.

'Will you make me come now?'

'Anything you want.'

Daphne unbuckled the leather ties that fastened the dildo around her waist, the length of it wet and shiny from Katy's juices, and lay where Katy had been lying previously, on the seat of the sofa. The blonde kissed her lover on the lips, then knelt on the floor in front of her and put her face between Daphne's legs, where the straps of the Black Betty had opened her pussy and made it as hot and wet as Katy's own, and Katy stuck her pink tongue up into the pink orifice as far as it would go and licked at the inside of Daphne's cavity.

Daphne opened her legs wide and allowed Katy's mouth free rein inside her, and the blonde lapped at Daphne's cunt like a kitten at a saucer of fresh cream. Bob looked on at this fresh depravity that his wife and her lover were partaking of with delight in his eyes, and he wanked his long cock until it was as hard as he had ever known it to be.

Daphne took hold of the fall of yellow hair at the back of Katy's head with both hands, and forced her face harder down onto the soot-coloured bush that Daphne loved to be cared for carnally by both men and women. Katy could hardly breathe, but still she licked and sucked at Daphne's labia until the brunette felt her own orgasm begin to grow inside her womb and burst like a skyrocket in her brain, and she closed her legs like scissors around Katy's head and ground her cunt into her lover's open mouth until she was satisfied.

The two women lay exhausted together until Daphne let go of the handfuls of Katy's hair that she still gripped in her fists and the blonde pulled away from the hot nest of Daphne's sex, only to see that Bob had got up from his chair and was removing his own clothing.

Katy watched as Bob stripped, and when he was naked he stood over the pair of naked females, exhibiting his muscular body proudly with his long cock standing out erect from the tangle of dark hair that covered his groin.

'It's my turn now,' he said. 'I want both of you. You first Katy.'

Katy was happy to accommodate him. Her cunt was ready for more sex and this time she wanted the spunk of a real man inside her, not the make-believe of an artificial cock, no matter how expertly it had been used, and she scrambled up onto the sofa next to Daphne and opened her legs wide as Bob covered her body with his. Without any fore-play he shoved his hot knob up into her slit.

Katy's gash was wide open and swallowed his lance of love easily, and she loved his weight on top of her and the masculine smell that exuded from his every pore, so different from the sweet perfume that had filled her nostrils as she had been shafted by his wife.

Bob moved his cock in and out of her willing pussy, and her cunt muscles gripped the length of him as they made love. His prick felt enormous inside her cunt and as his bollocks bounced against the twin orbs of her backside, she felt herself coming again, and she grabbed his shoulders and held on for dear life as another orgasm tore through her body.

Still erect, Bob withdrew from her cunt and said to Daphne, 'Come on darling. Your turn now. I want you to suck me off.'

'But I want your come,' begged Katy. 'I want to feel it hot and sticky, dripping out of me.'

'You will, my pet. Just have patience. But first I want my lovely wife to lick your lovely cunt juice off my John Thomas.'

He sat between the two girls and Daphne went down on his prick whilst Katy put her arms around him; they kissed deeply, his hands roving over her breasts and his wife's back as they formed a perfect threesome on the sofa.

'I must have your spunk,' Katy whispered in Bob's ear. 'Don't come in Daphne's mouth. Please.'

'I won't my darling,' he replied. 'I promise.'

Daphne pulled her mouth away from Bob's helmet and said, 'What are you two whispering about?'

'Katy wants my come,' said Bob. 'I've promised her a cuntful.'

'So do I,' said Daphne, 'I want to drink it.'

'And so you shall,' said Bob. 'You'll drink it out of Katy's pussy where I'm going to put it now.'

Katy almost fainted with relief, and almost creamed at the thought of Daphne drinking a come-cocktail from her gash. 'Yes, please,' she said, and slid down so that she was lying with her head on the arm of the sofa and her legs bent and open to expose her sex.

213

'How could I refuse such an invitation?' said Bob. 'Give me some room here, Daphne, I'm going to give your friend a good fucking.'

Pouting, Daphne did as she was told and perched on the other arm of the sofa as Bob mounted Katy again and began to beat at her body with his own. But Daphne didn't pout for long as she watched her husband and her female lover, who was now his too, moving together towards their mutual joyfulness. Instead she went over to the box she'd abandoned earlier and pulled out her vibrator, sat down where Bob had been sitting in the armchair, switched on the machine, and when it was humming to her satisfaction began to manipulate it on her clitoris as she watched the abandon of the pair screwing each other before her eyes.

Bob pounded at Katy harder and harder as he felt the first pulse of his orgasm deep in his balls, and she responded in kind as if she knew that soon she would be the vessel for his cream, waiting to shoot deep inside her. 'Come on, darling.' she cried, 'give it to me. I need it.'

'Yes, Katy,' he cried back. 'It's coming. Any second now . . .' And with a grunt he drove into her one last time and felt his hot stream of spunk shoot up the length of his cock and into her waiting femininity.

'Christ!' he bellowed as his cock continued spasming inside her. 'That was wonderful.'

Katy lay back with the weight of her new man on top of her, and looked over at Daphne whose eyes were closed as she too rocked with an orgasm, the length of the pink vibrator buried deep into the cleft between her legs.

Bob pulled himself out of Katy, and he too looked over at his wife. 'Come on, Daphne,' he said. 'I thought you wanted to lick my come out of Katy's cunt.'

'I do,' she replied, opening her eyes. 'I was just having a bit of fun on my own.'

'Well, come and join in now. You want her to lick you out, don't you Katy?'

Katy nodded. 'Oh yes,' she said.

Bob rolled off her naked body and stood up as his wife took his place, pulling Katy round and kneeling between her open legs and attaching her mouth to the lips of Katy's cunt. They were wide open too, after Bob's cock had pounded at them and deposited his semen inside.

As Daphne started to lick and suck the mixture of male and female come juice out of Katy's hole, Bob stepped into his boxer shorts, sat down in the arm-chair, picked up his drink and prepared himself to be entertained by the lesbian love scene enfolding before him.

Daphne's tongue felt delicious to Katy as it roamed around on her hairy mons, dipping into the openness of her cunt and licking out the mixture of her own and Bob's juice as it went, and the only sound she could hear in the room was the slurping sound that Daphne made as she drank the delicious love mixture that dribbled down Katy's love canal in through her greedy red lips.

Katy wanted the sensation to go on forever. For her just to lie there on her back on the sofa and for Daphne to explore her private parts until she was sucked dry.

But after ten or fifteen minutes of the beautiful attention, Daphne pulled her head back and said, 'I want to be fucked now.'

Bob was more than ready to oblige her. As he'd been watching his wife's dark head bobbing between Katy's milk white thighs and searching her blonde pubes for more delicious spunk to drink, his cock had grown in length and width again and he was ready to dip it in Daphne's love hole and give her the satisfaction that she craved.

At her words he stood up again, stripped off his shorts, pulled her away from Katy, lay her flat on the carpet and mounted her. Katy watched in wonderment as the two people who had loved her that night made love to each other. It was one of the most beautiful sights she had ever seen, and almost without thinking she put her hand down to the soaking hair between her legs, found her clit and started to play with it.

And as she watched, Bob and Daphne began to move faster on the carpeted floor. As she watched them moving towards mutual orgasm, she wanked her own clitoris harder so that as they came together on the floor, she came too, lying on her back on the sofa, watching them.

When Bob finally rolled off Daphne's supine form for the last time and helped her to her feet, all three of the lovers were exhausted. Bob put on his shorts again and poured fresh drinks as the two women got dressed. Then they all sat on the sofa together, their lust sated, and when Katy looked at her watch and saw the time, she got Bob to call her a cab which arrived ten minutes later. After warm, loving kisses all round she went out to the street, and the cabbie

216

drove her back to Waterloo where she found Mark fast asleep in bed. She undressed once more and crawled tiredly into it next to him, and soon fell into a deep sleep where she dreamt about all the fun she'd had that evening with Bob and Daphne.

PART THREE

37

On Friday afternoon, Katy caught the 14.39 to Folkestone from platform six at Charing Cross Station. She was dressed in what she thought could either be a business suit, or a going away outfit for the bride who took the business of marriage seriously. The previous lunchtime she'd gone to Harrods and spent far too much on a Dior suit in a mid-blue silk and wool mix that had a delicate sheen to the material, with a short skirt and a bolero jacket. She had teamed it with a pale pink silk blouse, so sheer that the lace of her white bra was visible through it, a white suspender belt, tiny white knickers with a lacey front that hardly covered her pubic hair, dark-blue, seamed stockings and high-heeled shoes whose colour exactly matched that of the suit. In the small bag she was carrying with her was a black negligee, an evening dress, a day dress, two changes of underwear, new stockings, both dark- and light-coloured and two pairs of shoes, along with her toilet and make-up bags. Over her arm was her Burberry, and all in all she felt that she was prepared for anything that the weekend might bring.

She got a seat at the front of the train, and as it pulled out of the station she opened the new Jilly

Cooper novel and settled down to enjoy the journey.

The train was dead on time at Folkestone Central Station, and as she walked through the ticket barrier she saw Sir Charles waiting outside on the pavement by the cab rank.

'My dear girl, you look delightful,' he said, kissing her on the cheek. 'The car is over there.'

Katy followed him to the Jaguar, where he put her case in the back with his own handsome leather luggage and opened the front passenger door for her before getting in behind the steering wheel.

'The hotel's on the front,' he said, 'We'll be there in a minute or two. Now you know I've booked the honeymoon suite, don't you?'

'Yes, Sir Charles,' said Katy breathlessly.

'So we're going to play a charade when we get there. You don't mind pretending to be my bride, do you?'

Katy shook her blonde mop that she'd spent nearly fifty pounds on the previous evening at one of the best salons in the West End.

'Then you'd better wear this,' he said and produced a gold wedding ring from one of the pockets in his jacket.

Katy was dumbfounded. 'It's beautiful,' she said.

'It belonged to my mother. Give me your hand.'

Katy could feel her whole body trembling as Sir Charles placed the ring on the third finger of her left hand. 'It fits perfectly. I knew it would.'

Katy held up her hand and admired the ring and wished that it was really hers.

'Do you like it?' asked Sir Charles.

'Of course I do.'

'Good. Then give me a kiss, you gorgeous thing, and let's get to the hotel, I can't wait to make love to you.'

Katy leant over and their mouths met, and she realised how much she'd missed Sir Charles since they'd last been together, and how much she was looking forward to their dirty weekend together.

When their lips parted Sir Charles started the car, put it into gear and swung it out of the station forecourt in the direction of the front. He'd been correct with his estimate of the distance, and within a few minutes he'd steered it through the imposing gates of the hotel and brought the Jaguar to a halt in front of a flight of stone steps that led up to the bank of doors allowing access to the foyer.

The doorman, resplendent in purple livery and sensing a large tip, came charging down the steps to open the car door.

'This is going to be fun,' said Sir Charles. 'Hold onto your hat dear girl,' and he laughed out loud, and when he did he looked twenty years younger. 'Now remember we just got married this morning. I expect you to be loving and attentive to your husband. Is that alright?'

Katy nodded as the doorman ushered her out of the car and took the keys from Sir Charles to rescue the luggage from the boot.

The trio trooped into hotel and up to the reception desk where a very snooty looking character in a black jacket, striped trousers and crisp white shirt and black tie peered over the top of his bifocals at them.

'Good afternoon, sir, madam,' he said. 'Can I be of any assistance?'

223

'My name is Wheeler,' said Sir Charles. 'I've booked the honeymoon suite for my wife and me.'

At this, Katy snuggled up close to Sir Charles, taking his arm in hers and smiling at the receptionist.

'Sir,' he said and punched the keys on the computer in front of him.

'Mr and Mrs Wheeler, of course,' then he looked down his nose at Sir Charles and Katy obviously, and correctly, surmising that they were a pair escaping from their responsibilities for a weekend in bed together.

'That's correct,' said Sir Charles. 'Married this morning in Maidenhead.'

Katy could hardly suppress a giggle. She had never realised that under his gruff exterior, Sir Charles was hiding a sense of humour.

'Of course, sir,' said the receptionist. 'If you'd just sign in.'

Sir Charles picked up a pen from the desk and filled in his name as straight Charles Wheeler, then with a flourish he took his handkerchief from his top pocket to mop his brow, and with it out flew a handful of scarlet confetti that drifted slowly to the carpet.

'My best man,' he explained to the goggle-eyed receptionist. 'Hell of a joker.'

Katy could stand it no longer and let forth a peel of laughter as the receptionist hit the bell on the desk in front of him to summon the porter to carry their luggage to Sir Charles and Katy's room.

'Thank you, my man,' Sir Charles said to the doorman and slipped him a five-pound note. 'What time is dinner?' he asked the receptionist who told him in a strangled voice that it was between the hours of seven and ten, before Sir Charles, Katy and the diminutive porter swept across the carpet to the lift.

The room the porter took them to was decorated in semi-gothic red plush and was dominated by a huge double bed covered in a red silk bedspread.

'This will do nicely,' said Sir Charles as the porter showed them the sitting room next door, complete with big screen TV and minibar stocked with champagne and miniatures of spirits and mixers, the view from the windows of the tide coming in across the seafront and the bathroom complete with jacuzzi. 'I'm sure we'll enjoy our few days here.'

38

When Sir Charles had tipped the porter with another five pound note, and he'd discreetly left the honeymoon suite, closing the door gently behind him, Katy laughed out loud. 'Oh Sir Charles, that was funny. When you pulled the confetti out of your pocket, I'm sure that convinced them.'

'Convinced them I was a cradle snatcher,' Sir Charles replied, and he too laughed at the thought of the receptionist's face.

'He was just jealous,' she said, taking off her jacket to reveal her breasts straining at the material of her blouse.

'And quite rightly so. Who wouldn't be jealous of any man who captured you for his bride?'

'Oh, Sir Charles,' said Katy, blushing prettily.

'Don't you think you could call me Charles now. At least in private.'

'Oh, Sir Charles,' said Katy. 'May I?'

'Of course you may. I am your husband after all.'

Katy smiled at him. 'So you are,' she said, and blushed again. If only he were, she thought for one giddy moment.

'Do you like the idea?' he teased.

She nodded, and she felt the blush spread all over her body, centring on the sticky mess she was oozing between her legs at being alone with Sir Charles in the honeymoon suite of an expensive hotel.

'There's only one thing you haven't done,' she said.

Sir Charles looked puzzled. 'What?' he asked.

'Carried me over the threshold.'

'I didn't know if the porter would approve,' he replied. 'But I'll do it now if you want me to.'

'No. It's alright,' said Katy.

'Do you think I'm too old and weak.'

'Of course not.'

'Come on then.' And he grabbed her hand and pulled her towards the door.

'What if someone's outside.'

'What if they are? We're on our honeymoon. We're allowed to play the fool.'

He opened the door of the suite and they went outside into the deserted corridor. Sir Charles smiled and picked Katy up as if she weighed no more than a feather. She felt his left hand under her skirt on her thighs, bare except for the straps of her suspenders, whilst his other arm was round her waist. Instinctively she put her arm around his shoulders and nestled against his strong chest as he carried her back into the room and slammed the door behind them with his foot. Their faces were close and he said, 'Is that what you wanted.'

Katy smiled and nodded.

'Then kiss your husband,' said Sir Charles.

Katy did as he said, parting her lips, and Sir Charles did the same and their tongues flicked into each other's mouths.

Their kiss was long and slow and sensuous, but couldn't last long enough for Katy.

They broke from each other for a moment and Sir Charles whispered, 'Shall we consummate the marriage?'

Katy felt her stomach drop as if she was in an express lift up to Heaven. 'Consummate,' she whispered, 'what a beautiful word.'

'So shall we?'

'Please, darling,' she said, even getting a sexual charge from calling this powerful man by a love name.

He picked her up again, as if she was a feather and carried her over to the bed where he deposited her gently onto the red silk cover, then stood back and began to undress.

Katy watched as if mesmerised. Here she was, a seventeen-year-old junior secretary who her boss had already passed off as his wife, and was undressing in front of her in the honeymoon suite of a grand hotel, before treating her like one.

Her cunt lubricated like Niagara Falls, and her juice was rushing out of her love tunnel and down her bare thighs. There was so much that for a moment it felt as if she'd been fucking all day instead of being about to fuck all night.

Sir Charles pulled off his tie and unbuttoned his shirt. Underneath he wore a snowy white T-shirt of very fine cotton. He took off his shirt and pulled the T-shirt over his head.

He kicked off his loafers and swiftly pulled off his socks, then unfastened the button at the top of his trousers and slid down the zip of the fly. He pushed his trousers over his hips and allowed them to drop to the floor and stepped out of them. Under his trousers he was wearing youthfully cut, close-fitting, blue and white striped boxer shorts, the material of which his erect penis jutted through like the nose of a jet fighter.

Katy loved this further proof of his desire for her. No wonder all the women fancied him. She almost salivated at the sight of his cock poking through his pants. In fact her cunt *did* salivate, and if she thought it felt like Niagara Falls before, now it felt as if the Pacific Ocean was pouring out of her quim.

He sat on the bed next to her and undid the buttons on her blouse to reveal the half cups of her lacey white bra, and she shrugged her top garment back.

'Virginal white,' he whispered.

'A knight's bride should always be a virgin, shouldn't she?'

'And are you?'

'For you I am.'

He smiled down at her and finished unbuttoning her blouse and tugged it from the waistband of her skirt, pulling it off her back, and dropping it onto the bed. Then he found the zip at the side of her skirt, pulled it down and Katy wriggled the garment down her legs and tossed it onto the floor. Sir Charles looked down the length of her body and she felt herself blush. Her breasts were overflowing from the tiny bra cups that struggled to contain the twin white beauties with their strawberry sorbet-coloured nipples, and the material of her brief knickers hardly covered her sex.

'You are beautiful,' he said.

'Do you really think so?'

'Of course,' he replied, and lowered his mouth to hers, and they kissed for the second time, even more lingeringly than the first time, if that were possible.

Sir Charles's hand went to Katy's left breast and he fondled it through the material of her bra until she was breathless under his tantalising fingers and lips.

'Take it off, darling,' she said, and his hands moved round to the fastener at the back, and within seconds her breasts were bare and he laid her back on the soft silk bedcover and moved his mouth down to first one nipple, then the other until they were both wet and hard, and Katy's cunt was begging to be penetrated by her lover.

She put her fingers down to the elastic of her panties, pushed them over her hips, down her legs and kicked them off, then boldly pulled down Sir Charles's boxer shorts so that he was naked before her, and she was naked before him except for her stockings and suspenders.

When he put his hand between her legs he said, 'Wench, you're soaking.'

'It's just for you my husband,' she whispered. 'Come inside me.'

'I want you on top,' he said, and lay down on the bed and Katy climbed onto his body, found the tip of his enormous prick, put it into her slit and slowly slid down the length of it, loving the feeling of being speared by the beautiful piece of meat between Sir Charles's legs.

When he was all the way in she slowly lowered her upper body onto his and they kissed passionately as Katy rode up and down on his cock.

'I want your spunk, darling,' she said. 'I want to

230

feel it running out of me all night long.'

'And you shall have it my love,' he said. 'Every drop in my balls.'

'It can't be enough,' she whispered. 'I want to drown in the lovely stuff.'

At her words she felt Sir Charles's cock twitch inside her and she knew that soon she would feel the hot jet of his sperm inside her, and she drove down on him harder and faster, her breasts flattened against his chest.

'Let me get on top,' he said, and they rolled over together, still joined at the groin. Sir Charles took control of the fuck, and Katy gave herself totally to him as he pounded his hard body against her softness. She entwined her long legs around his back and rasped the soft nylon over his buttocks and thighs.

'You're mine,' she whispered as he shafted his cock in and out of her cunt.

'Yes, my gorgeous whore,' he said.

'I love being your whore. I love being your tart.'

'The most beautiful tart in the world,' he gasped as his strokes got shorter. 'And there's nothing better than a tart in the bedroom and a lady out of it.'

'Am I a lady?'

'Yes my darling, why do you think I asked you away for this weekend? So that I could show off the most beautiful lady in the place on my arm, and see her turn into a slut when we're alone.'

'Then shoot your slut. Give her your love,' said Katy, and her excitement was so intense that she came hard onto his cock, which drove Sir Charles to a fresh frenzy of fucking until he could control himself no longer and she felt the jet of come burst inside her.

He slumped on top of her body, their hot sweat mingling on their skin.

'Wonderful,' he said, 'truly wonderful.'

After they had lain together for a few minutes, Sir Charles withdrew his cock from Katy's hole and he rolled off her and lay breathing heavily with his arms across her body.

'Consummation,' he said.

39

Eventually Sir Charles looked over at his watch and said, 'Care for a drink before dinner?'

'I'd love one,' said Katy.

'Then let's get dressed and go to the bar. I told you I want to show you off and I shall.'

'And I told you I want to feel your come squeezing out of me all night,' said Katy. 'I'm not going to shower or wear any undies.'

'I knew you were a dirty little slut,' said Sir Charles. 'And if you don't wear any knickers I'm going to want to touch your bottom all night long.'

'As my husband you have my full permission,' said Katy.

Sir Charles *did* shower, but Katy refused to go into the bathroom with him in case he dragged her in and ruined not only her resolution to stay dirty, but her new hair-do as well. Instead she stayed in the bedroom and got ready on her own.

It didn't take long. All she wore was the little black cocktail dress she had brought with her, a pair of sheer hold-up stockings with lace around the tops and black, high-heeled shoes. And by the time Sir Charles emerged from the bathroom wearing the complimentary robe supplied by the hotel and towelling his hair, Katy was in the sitting room watching the news on the television and sipping a gin and tonic she'd prepared from the supplies in the minibar.

'I see you're in the mood,' said Sir Charles.

'Aren't I always?'

'Stand up. Let me look at you.'

Katy did as he said, and he came close. 'You look wonderful. That's a very attractive dress.'

'Thank you, sir,' she said and did a twirl, but as he came closer she said. 'Don't touch me, you'll get white bits all over the material and I'll never get them off.'

'Yes, Madam,' he said with a grin. 'Anything you say. I'll get dressed, then I'll get close.'

'You'll be very welcome,' she said, and he went back into the bedroom.

When he reappeared he was wearing a fresh dark suit, a clean shirt and Garrick Club tie.

'Now come here,' he said, and Katy went straight into his arms.

'Did you put on any knickers?' he asked.

'That's for me to know and you to find out.'

Sir Charles put his hand down to the hem of her skirt and ran it up her leg past the tops of her stockings into the heat and wet of her cunt where the juices from their fuck were running deliciously out of her still-open pussy and down her thighs.

'You didn't did you?' he said.

'I told you I wouldn't.'

'You temptress.'

'I know. Now how about that drink?'

'Are you sure you wouldn't rather go back to bed?'

'Quite sure. I'm starving.'

'I'm starving for you.'

'Then you'll have to wait until after dinner. But you've got my full permission to feel me up as much as you want during the meal.'

'And I will.'

And he did.

40

Katy and Sir Charles went down to the bar which was situated next to the hotel restaurant, and although it was relatively early, there was still quite a crowd in the room and every head turned as the handsome knight entered with the beautiful blonde teenager on his arm, obviously infatuated with the older man. They took a booth in a dark corner and Sir Charles ordered a bottle of champagne.

'Come here, my darling,' he said when the waiter had gone. 'I want to put my hand up your skirt again.'

'You are bold,' said Katy.

'With a horny wench like you next to me, who wouldn't be?' he said. 'Now come here.'

Katy slithered over the leather of her banquette and Sir Charles put his hand on her knee, then slid her skirt up her legs as she looked him straight in the eye. 'I hope no one can see,' she said.

'I don't care if they can.'

'Oh, Charles,' she said, as he touched a particularly sensitive spot on the inside of her leg.

'Does that feel good?' he asked.

'Yes. Does it feel good to you?'

'Wonderful,' he replied as his hand once again found

the smooth, naked skin of her thighs and pushed her skirt ever higher until once again he plunged his fingers into the coiling wetness that bubbled from her youthful pussy.

As his fingers found the entrance to her hair hole, the waiter re-appeared with the champagne. Sir Charles used his other hand to pick up his glass and taste the wine whilst he fingered Katy's quim; she tried to keep from wriggling around on her seat under the dark eyes of the handsome waiter.

'Perfect,' said Sir Charles when he had savoured the ice-cold bubbly. 'Pour my wife a glass.'

'Of course, sir,' said the waiter, and he filled Katy's glass. With shaking fingers she picked it up as Sir Charles dug deeper into her soft private parts.

'That's lovely,' she said, and only Sir Charles could guess that she wasn't referring to her drink alone.

After the waiter had left them alone again. Sir Charles withdrew his fingers from under her skirt, dipped them into Katy's glass before sensually licking the mixture of champagne and cunt juice off them with his tongue.

'You make me feel young again, Katy Dunn,' he said. 'And for that I'll be forever grateful.'

'I'm glad,' she replied. 'You make me feel like a real woman. Something that young men can never do.'

'Then I'm glad too. Drink up and we'll get the waiter to bring the bottle into the restaurant. Much as I love showing you off in here, I'd rather be upstairs in bed with you.'

'Me too,' said Katy.

When they'd both emptied their glasses, they got up from the booth and walked together over to the bar, where the small crowd fell silent as Sir Charles instructed the barman to bring their bottle and fresh glasses into the restaurant where they were going to eat.

They sat at a secluded table and Sir Charles said, 'I told you everyone would envy me.'

'And I think the women envied me,' said Katy.

'Flatterer.'

'It's the truth.'

'We seem to fit together well.'

'I think so.'

'So do I.'

Katy couldn't believe her ears. What, she wondered, was Sir Charles leading up to?

'Shall we order,' he asked, picking up the menu. 'I'm starving.'

41

When they got back up to the room, Katy immediately took her black negligee into the bathroom. There she took off her dress and hung it behind the door before sliding into the lace creation she had taken with her, leaving her stockings and high-heeled shoes on beneath it. Finally, she freshened her make-up in the mirror above the washbasin, and once satisfied went back into the suite and found Sir Charles in the sitting room with an opened bottle of champagne on the table in front of him.

When Katy came through the door from the bedroom her figure was silhouetted in the doorway by the light behind her, and Sir Charles could clearly see every curve of her beautiful body through the fine black material of her nightdress.

'You look lovely, darling,' he said. 'Drink?'

'Love one.'

Sir Charles poured cold wine into a chilled flute as she walked towards him. She knew how desirable she looked in the negligee. Mark had told her enough times, and when she was alone she often put it on in front of the mirror in her room and wondered what Sir Charles would think if he ever saw her in it.

And now he could, and the way it showed off every hollow and plain of her pure white body through the thin material seemed to be having the desired effect.

Katy sat next to Sir Charles on the sofa, they toasted each other and drank.

'I think I'm falling for you,' said Sir Charles. 'No woman has had this effect on me for years.'

'I've already fallen for you,' said Katy boldly. 'I did the first time we made love.'

'I think I was rather cruel to you.'

'I don't mind as long as it's you that's doing it.'

'Is that right?'

Katy nodded, and they kissed. When they broke apart Sir Charles took Katy's glass from her hand and put it next to his on the table. 'I want you,' he whispered.

'Then take me. I'm ready.'

Sir Charles took Katy in his arms and they kissed again. He put his hand to her breast and felt her nipple hard against his palm through the sheer material of her negligee. Then he put his hand down on the hem of her garment and flipped it over her thighs. Katy pulled it up further to display her naked cunt, still dripping from their previous love making, the remains of which had left a wet transparent coating on the insides of her thighs.

'I want to drink our love juice,' said Sir Charles breathlessly.

Katy opened her legs, and he knelt between them on the carpet and put his face down into her blonde bush.

She lay back as he lapped at the open hole and felt herself lubricating again as she listened to the slurping of Sir Charles's tongue on the lips of her pussy.

When he'd drunk his fill he came up onto the sofa again and his and Katy's mouths met once more, and Katy licked and sucked their juices from his mouth, making little satisfied noises in the back of her throat as she did it.

Sir Charles gently lay Katy back onto the cushions of the sofa and pushed her negligee up until the skirt at the front of it was under her chin, and the rest of the garment fanned out around her making her skin seem even whiter, apart from the rosy nipples on her breasts. The sight almost drove Sir Charles to distraction.

He stood up and tore off his clothing until he was naked and rampant above her, and as she watched him she put her hand down to her slit, opened it and played with her engorged clitoris.

Sir Charles looked down at her, then lay beside her. They kissed again, thankful that at last they had the time to explore each other fully. Sir Charles marvelled, not for the first time, at Katy's flawless body, and she admired his muscular physique; it appeared to belong to a much younger man.

Sir Charles put his head down and kissed Katy's breasts, spending long minutes sucking her nipples until they were red and raw under his ministrations, but Katy loved the feeling of his lips on the hard nubs at the tops of her breasts, and as he sucked she stroked his cock and gently massaged his hard bollocks.

When he'd finished his exploration of Katy's tits, Sir Charles put his hand down into the hair between her legs and she smiled, knowing that soon she and her lover would couple, and be one again.

Almost immediately Sir Charles climbed onto Katy's supine body, and she felt the knob of his prick at the entrance to her pussy. She reached down and guided it in and Sir Charles bore down heavily on her so that she felt the great length of it slide up her love canal.

Sir Charles had never felt as much a part of a woman as he did with Katy, for all his experience of sex, and she, in her own way, had never felt so taken over by a man as she did when Sir Charles was part of her.

The pair moved together perfectly, feeling every inch of each other's bodies with their own as Sir Charles slid his cock in and out of Katy's cunt and she moved her hips beneath him.

'Rock me,' he said, 'in the cradle of your love,' and Katy moved faster and felt the heat of his prick all the way up her cunt and into her womb.

As Katy moved beneath her lover she could feel the hardness of his balls banging against her arse and his chest coming down on hers and flattening her breasts as their hard nipples collided. She thought that the feeling was wonderful, and she cried out loud as her first orgasm rocked her whole body. Nothing could be better than that she thought, but when Sir Charles stiffened above her and shot the hot, milky fluid from his stiff prick right up into the very centre of her being she came again, and this time her screams of passion were even louder.

42

That night they made love on the sofa again. On the carpet in the sitting room. In the shower, and twice in the huge honeymoon bed.

They made love all evening and half the night, and Katy woke late, and lay on her back next to her sleeping lover with her cunt still sore from their exertions, but feeling wonderful. Sated with sex for the moment, but experiencing a slight tingling in her pussy at the feel of Sir Charles's arm laying loosely across her body.

'Charles, darling,' she said.

He rolled over and mumbled something she couldn't understand.

'Charles,' she said again and shook him, and his eyes opened.

'Katy,' he said. 'I was just dreaming about you.'

'Were you?'

'Yes. And now here you are, and may I say, looking like an angel this morning.'

'Do you think so?'

'I do. Can't you tell?'

In fact she could as she felt Sir Charles's manhood swelling up against her leg, and wonderful it felt too.

'Yes, darling,' she said reaching for him. 'But aren't you a bit sore? I am.'

'Just a little, but a slow dip in the ointment between your legs will make me feel better.'

'Then get in,' she said. 'I want to hold you inside me again.'

Sir Charles didn't waste a moment, and he mounted Katy without another word and she slid the top of his knob into her gash. Ever so slowly she swallowed him up inside her, and the soreness between her legs vanished to be replaced with a sweet and tingling pleasure.

'That's wonderful,' she said. 'Just what I needed.'

'Me, too,' replied Sir Charles, beginning to move ever so slowly inside her. 'How does that feel?'

'Delicious. Like peaches and cream.'

'My peach,' he said, 'your cream.'

'Is your peach full of juice?'

'Very.'

'Then squeeze some into me.'

'It'll be my pleasure.'

'And mine.'

'I hope so.'

'I know so.'

With that, Sir Charles began to move slightly faster, then faster still until he clenched his face in concentration and, with an expellation of breath, shot his seed into Katy again.

'I didn't come,' she complained when he was spent.

'My poor darling. Shall I see what I can do about that?'

'Yes, please,' and Sir Charles rolled off his teenage lover and straightaway put his fingers down into the thatch between her legs and found her clitoris peeping out cheekily from between the folds of skin at the mouth of her vagina.

He pinched it gently between his fingers and Katy quivered with every fibre of her body and put her hand on his chest.

'Is that good?' he asked.

'Wonderful. Do it some more.'

He did as she asked and waves of pleasure rocked her being and she drummed her heels on the mattress.

Sir Charles kept on playing with her cunt until she could bear it no longer and she screamed out loud, gripped his hand with hers, forcing it down harder onto her mound of Venus and came.

She lay there as Sir Charles kissed and cuddled her, then he said. 'I'm sorry to be so mundane, my darling, but if you want breakfast we should go soon.'

'Can't we have breakfast in bed?' pleaded Katy.

'Not this morning. Tomorrow. I need to talk to you and I can't do it when we're in bed together. I want you dressed and separated from me by a table. I can't keep my hands off you otherwise.'

'I'm flattered,' said Katy. 'But I'd rather stay here.'

'Don't you want to hear what I've got to say?'

Sir Charles sounded so serious that Katy sat up in bed immediately. 'Of course. Let me get a quick shower and I'll be with you.'

'Let me go first,' said Sir Charles. 'I know you and hot water. Then I'll get downstairs and capture a table and make sure they don't close the restaurant.'

Sir Charles kissed Katy again briefly, got out of bed and went into the bathroom where he showered and shaved. He came back into the bedroom and dressed quickly, then kissed Katy again and left the suite.

She got up then, went to the bathroom, showered, cleaned her teeth and put on minimum make-up, all the time wondering what Sir Charles was going to say. She went back into the bedroom slipped into bra, panties, the day dress she'd brought with her and high-heeled pumps, then let herself out of the suite and went down to the restaurant to join him. The room was almost deserted when she arrived, and Sir Charles was sitting at a table for two by the window.

'Are we in time?' asked Katy, seeing that the few remaining diners were finishing their meals and leaving.

'Of course,' said Sir Charles, sipping at his orange juice. 'It's amazing what service a fiver will get you.'

'Did you tip the waitress a fiver?'

'Yes,' said Sir Charles. 'I couldn't bear the thought of her glowering at us as we're eating.'

'You're wonderful,' breathed Katy.

'I wonder if you'll think so when you've heard what I've got to say to you.'

'What is it?'

Sir Charles reached over and took Katy's hand. 'My permanent secretary, Lorraine, is coming back to the office.'

'What?'

'Yes. She's fully recovered now and she's coming back on Monday week. So you see I won't have a vacancy for a temp any more, after that.'

'You mean . . . ?'

'Yes. I'm afraid you won't be my secretary any more after next Friday.'

'Charles.' That was all Katy could say. She was

devastated. Eventually she stuttered. 'So is that why you brought me here? To tell me that?'

He smiled. 'Partly. But there is something else.'

'What?'

'Another vacancy *has* come up.'

'As what?' said Katy. 'Tea lady?'

'Well, it's a lady, and that's a fact. But not a tea lady.'

'What then?'

'As *Lady* Wheeler. My wife.'

Katy couldn't believe what she was hearing. 'Are you serious?' she asked.

'Never more so.'

'Are you asking me to marry you?'

Sir Charles nodded and squeezed her fingers harder.

'You used to sleep with Lorraine, didn't you?' Katy said eventually.

'Whoever told you that?'

'A little bird. Is it true?'

Sir Charles hesitated, then shrugged and nodded. 'Yes.'

'Then I will marry you. On one condition.'

'Which is?'

'That you get rid of her and let me choose a new secretary for you.'

'Anyone in mind?'

'Someone old and unattractive.'

Sir Charles beamed. 'If you say so,' he said. 'But if you do marry me, have you thought what your boyfriend and family will say?'

'I'll take care of them,' said Katy. 'Don't you worry about that.'

And she did.

43

Katy Dunn became Lady Charles Wheeler in a quiet ceremony at Marylebone registry officer later that summer. Her mother, father and brother attended. Cousin Mark did not. Daphne was her maid of honour. Katy and Daphne spent the night before the wedding in a suite at the Savoy where they made passionate love, and where the next morning amidst much jollity they dressed each other, then made love again wearing their wedding outfits before leaving for the function.

Sir Charles made a handsome bridegroom, and Katy looked beautiful in her short white dress, with matching accessories, carrying a huge bouquet of white roses with just one red bloom for contrast. Sir Charles's new secretary, a strict forty-seven-year-old, unmarried Scots woman, had arranged the occasion with the same ruthless efficiency that she showed in his office. Sir Charles's previous secretary having been transferred to the oil company offices in Aberdeen at Katy's insistence.

After the wedding breakfast which was held in a private room back at the Savoy, the happy couple honeymooned for a week in Paris and a week in Barbados before they returned to London and took up residence in a town house in Eaton Square, where Lady Wheeler, despite her youth and inexperience, soon became a leading light in metropolitan society.

A selection of bestsellers
from Headline